Lee's always been the best . . . until now

Before the girl threw her next punch, Lee concentrated on her feet. He was trying to catch her in a mistake. Her foot moved forward, all right. Her fist came right after it, like a blur, landing squarely on Lee's solar plexus.

"Aaahh!" Lee gasped as he took the blow. His forearms had been nowhere near his chest at that time. The pain in his solar plexus was so sharp he could barely breathe.

D1016742

When you seek it, you cannot find it.
—Zen riddle

KARATE CLUB

Girl Trouble

CARIN GREENBERG BAKER

PUFFIN BOOKS

*This book is dedicated to Master Ansei Ueshiro
who brought Shorin-Ryu karate
to the United States in 1962.*

PUFFIN BOOKS
Published by the Penguin Group
Penguin Books USA Inc.,
375 Hudson Street, New York, New York 10014, U.S.A.
Penguin Books Ltd, 27 Wrights Lane, London W8 5TZ, England
Penguin Books Australia Ltd, Ringwood, Victoria, Australia
Penguin Books Canada Ltd, 10 Alcorn Avenue, Toronto, Ontario, Canada M4V 3B2
Penguin Books (N.Z.) Ltd, 182–190 Wairau Road, Auckland 10, New Zealand

Penguin Books Ltd, Registered Offices: Harmondsworth, Middlesex, England

First published in the United States of America by Puffin Books,
a division of Penguin Books USA Inc., 1992
1 3 5 7 9 10 8 6 4 2

Library of Congress Catalog Card Number: 91-68482
ISBN: 0-14-036074-3

Printed in the United States of America
Set in Bookman

Chapter One

"Gimme a break!" Lee Jenkins shouted as he eyed the piece of paper his younger brother, Jeremy, had just shoved into his hands. "Nobody gets a hundred and *five* on a science test. A hundred is the highest you can get."

"Not anymore," Jeremy said proudly as the two walked down the crowded hallway. Classes at Midvale Middle School were over for the day. Now other sixth graders like Lee and Jeremy rushed past in both directions, laughing, yelling, and slamming their lockers.

"Mr. Frazier said it was a new record for his class," Jeremy bragged. "I got all the answers right, *plus* the extra credit question, *plus* I found a mistake in the way he set up one of the problems so he gave me two extra points for that."

Lee shook his head in disbelief, and his shiny black bangs fell into his eyes. He'd always known Jeremy was an unbelievable brain when it came to science and math, but this was ridiculous! Not that Lee was jealous or anything. His own grades were pretty good. He got mostly B's, which was fine with him. He didn't want to grow up to be a famous scientist the way Jeremy did.

Lee wanted to open his own *dojo,* or karate school, when he grew up. He didn't need top grades for that. What he needed was a black belt in karate, and he was well on his way to that already. Lee was only twelve, but he'd already earned his brown belt. He was the most advanced of the young students at the Midvale Karate Dojo. He, Jeremy, and their older brother, Michael, were all enrolled at the dojo, and spent many days after school there.

In less than a week, Lee might advance even further. This coming Sunday was the big promotion where students could test for the next rank. Lee was planning to test for his black tips. Black tips was a very advanced rank, just one level short of black belt. There were only a few adult students at the dojo who had black tips. To have black tips as a kid was a pretty big deal.

"Good job, Jer," Lee said, handing the science test back to Jeremy. "Just don't forget, when you build the first rocket ship for intergalactic space travel, save me a seat."

Jeremy grinned, crinkling his freckled nose. His red hair stood out a little from his head, and his blue eyes blinked behind round, wire-rimmed glasses. "I can see it now," Jeremy said. "You'll be the *sensei* of the first intergalactic dojo." *Sensei,* the Japanese word for teacher, was what they called their karate instructor. Instead of saying 'Mr. Davis,' they said 'Sensei Davis.'

Lee pushed open the back door of the sixth grade wing. It was a bright autumn day. Crackly brown leaves swirled in the chilly breeze. Behind the school was a long rack where Lee and his brothers always parked their bicycles.

Michael was there already, spinning the combination on his bike lock. Tall and athletic, Michael had straight blond hair and brown eyes. He was thirteen and in eighth grade. Even though he was older, Michael wasn't as advanced in karate as Lee. Michael had a green belt with brown tips. That was partly because Michael had started karate a year after Lee had. Jeremy, who'd started even later, had a green belt.

"Hey, Michael!" Jeremy called, waving his science test. "Take a look at this!"

Michael took the paper and looked at it. "A hundred and *five*? That's *all*?" he teased. "Better not show it to Mom and Dad."

"Are you kidding?" Jeremy asked, unlocking his bike. "They're going to buy a solid gold frame for it. And they're going to buy a second gold frame for my certificate."

"What certificate?" Lee asked, slipping his arms

through the shoulder straps of his blue knapsack so he'd be ready for their bike ride to the dojo. Today, like every Monday, Lee and his brothers took the after-school karate class for kids.

"My karate promotion certificate!" Jeremy said. "The one saying I've earned my brown tips."

Lee was surprised. Jeremy had only earned his green belt six months ago, at the last promotion. He wasn't anywhere near ready to test. But Jeremy was always in a hurry to prove himself. "Slow down," Lee warned his brother. "You have to get permission to test from Sensei Davis first. We all do."

Sensei Davis was a third-degree black belt and owner of the Midvale Karate Dojo. Lee was planning to ask for his permission today, right after karate class.

"I'll get permission," Jeremy said confidently.

"I wish I felt as sure as you do," Michael told Jeremy as the three of them backed their bicycles onto the sidewalk. Michael wanted to test for his brown belt. Lee was pretty sure Michael would get permission. Michael had been a green belt with brown tips for a year and a half, and his techniques were looking good. Still, it was up to Sensei. Students often thought they were ready before they really were. Sensei didn't give permission to everyone who asked. What if Sensei said no to all three of them?

"Let's try not to think about it," Lee said, hopping on his bike. "It's up to Sensei Davis, not us."

Jeremy started pedaling slowly towards the opening in the chain link fence that surrounded the school. "How can we *not* think about it? Anyway, we should have our answer right after class."

Lee and Michael caught up with Jeremy. After they passed through the gate they turned right onto the main road.

Michael groaned. "Even if we do get permission, it's still scary. Think of all the people who'll be watching."

Much as Lee wanted to test, he wasn't looking forward to that part. Every time there was a promotion, karate students, or *deshi*, came from all over the country to watch. There were over a dozen dojo in the United States that studied the same style of karate Lee and his brothers did. There was one in Philadelphia, one in North Carolina, even one in Hawaii! Some of the deshi were high-ranking black belts, and they often sat on the review board that judged the students who were testing.

Lee had heard a rumor that Sensei Modigliani, Sensei Davis's teacher, would be coming. Sensei Modigliani was a fifth-degree black belt and owned the dojo in North Carolina where Sensei Davis had studied before he moved to Midvale.

"I don't care how many people are watching me!" Jeremy called, racing ahead of them down the hill. "All I care about is getting to class, 'cause the sooner we get there, the sooner we'll get the good news!"

* * *

A few minutes later, Lee checked his reflection in the full-length mirror that hung on the wall in the men's locker room. Small and wiry, he was already dressed in his white cotton karate uniform, called a *gi*. His brown belt was tied around his waist. Since his straight black hair was always falling into his eyes, he'd also tied a red bandana around his forehead. His almond-shaped eyes were dark brown.

Lee, who was Vietnamese, had been adopted by the Jenkins family when he was five years old. Lee still remembered Vietnam and his grandfather, who'd taken care of Lee after his parents had died when he was just a baby. Lee could also remember the orphanage where he'd lived after his grandfather died. Luckily, he hadn't stayed there long. Stephen Jenkins, who'd been a U.S. soldier in the Vietnam war, and his wife, Andrea, had adopted him and brought him home to live with their family.

All that had happened such a long time ago that Lee hardly ever thought about it. His adoptive parents and brothers always treated him like he'd been born into the family, and Lee felt that way, too.

Lee tightened the knot of his belt, then headed for the door that led to the karate classroom. Pulling aside the curtain that covered the doorway, Lee stepped onto the polished wooden floor, also called the deck.

The room was large and square. The front wall of

6

the dojo, the *shinden* wall, was decorated with two large flags, one of the United States and the other— all white with a large round dot in the center—the flag of Japan.

Between the two flags were black-and-white photographs of the shinden or karate masters. At the far left were the teachers from Okinawa, the tiny island between Japan and China where karate first began. Then there was a picture of Ansei Ueshiro, the Okinawan master who'd brought their style of karate to the United States. Next was a picture of Sensei Modigliani from North Carolina, who'd studied under Master Ueshiro and who'd also taught Sensei Davis. Last was a picture of Sensei Davis. Lee loved the way karate passed from one person to another, from the distant past to the present, so that he was linked to the ancient karate masters of long ago.

There were only a few minutes until class was supposed to start, so the deck was already filling up with kids in their gi. After five years at the dojo, Lee knew nearly all of them.

Rosalie Davis, Sensei's daughter, stood in the back of the class punching the *makiwara*, a wooden post with thick rope wrapped around it. By punching the makiwara, you toughened your knuckles and learned how to keep your fists tight. Rosalie was also a brown belt, but ranked just under Lee because she'd been promoted six months after him.

7

Michael and Jeremy were practicing *kata* with Dwight Vernon and Jon Walker, two of the other green belts. A kata was a choreographed sequence of blocking and attacking techniques fought against an imaginary opponent. By practicing a kata over and over again, the moves became instinctive. If you were ever attacked in a street fight, the moves from kata would come to you without thinking.

You'd never use those moves to attack anyone first, of course. The first rule everyone learned when they started karate was *karate ni sente nashi*. There is no first attack in karate.

The four green belts moved in sync as they dropped into low cat stances, their weight supported on bent back legs with their front legs resting lightly on the floor in front of them.

Kevin Whittaker, a white belt who'd recently earned his first green tip, squatted in front of the mirror punching an imaginary opponent.

"Hyaaaaah!"

Every time Kevin's fist shot out in front of him, he gave a loud *kiai*.

"Hyaaaaah!"

Kiai was a shout used to startle your opponent, but it was also a way of focusing all your energy and power into one sharp burst.

Lee started to head towards the back to take turns with Rosalie on the makiwara. Then he noticed a new white-belt student standing shyly by the mirrored wall, looking confused and lost. The boy looked about nine or ten years old, with pink-white skin and blond hair. His brand new gi still had the creases in it from the way it had been folded in the package, and his white belt was tied wrong.

Lee headed for the blond boy, taking a detour around the red plastic bucket catching drips from the leaky ceiling. As a senior student, it was Lee's responsibility to work with new white belts, teach them the basic techniques, and make them feel comfortable at the dojo.

"*Onegai-shimasu,*" Lee said, bowing.

The blond boy smiled nervously at Lee. Lee could tell he didn't have the slightest idea what Lee had just said.

"Onegai-shimasu means 'please teach me' in Japanese," Lee explained. "Whenever you work with another deshi, a karate student, that's what you say. I say it to you and you say it to me. Onegai-shimasu."

"But how can I teach you?" the boy said. "Today's my first day. You're a brown belt."

"Anybody can learn from anybody else," Lee said. "It doesn't matter what rank you have. Try it. Onegai-shimasu."

"Omy gosh moss," the boy said, mispronouncing the words and bowing awkwardly.

"I'm Lee Jenkins," Lee introduced himself.

9

"Timothy, I mean Tim, Unruh," the boy said.

"Let's work some basic techniques in front of the mirror," Lee said, leading the boy to the mirrored wall where Kevin Whittaker was still punching and making faces. Kevin shifted over so Lee and Timothy could have more room.

"I have to warn you," Timothy said. "I've never done this stuff before. I'm not any good."

"Don't worry about whether you're good or not," Lee advised him. "Everybody feels clumsy their first day. But you'll get over it real fast. You'll see."

"I hope so," Tim said, looking doubtful.

"Let's start with a basic chest block," Lee said. He positioned himself so that he was facing Tim. "A chest block is to protect you when someone is aiming a punch at your solar plexus. That's the nerve center right below the rib cage and one of the most vulnerable targets on the body."

Very slowly, Lee aimed his right fist at Tim's solar plexus, just so Tim could see where it was.

"Now," Lee said, shifting around so he was standing next to Tim, looking in the mirror, "the first thing you do when someone throws a punch there is cover like this." Lee crossed his forearms over his solar plexus so that they made an X across his chest. His hands were clenched into fists, thumbs in tight against his shoulders.

Tim tried to copy Lee, also making an X.

10

"That's good," Lee encouraged him. "That means the only thing your opponent hit was your arms. They're a lot tougher and bonier than your chest."

Tim nodded in understanding.

"The next thing you do," Lee said, "is deflect the punch." Lee's left arm was on the outside of the X. Now he twisted it sideways, turning his arm so his fist was up in front of his shoulder. At the same time, Lee brought his right elbow straight back, ending when his right fist was even with his ribs. This was called putting the fist "in the pocket."

Tim flicked his left arm out, but he forgot to turn it.

"Try it again," Lee counseled. "You want to twist the arm to add more power. You'll see that twist in almost every technique."

Tim nodded and did the block again correctly.

"Good!" Lee complimented him. "You're getting the hang of it already."

"I don't know," Tim said, looking worried. "I feel so . . . dumb!"

"You're not," Lee assured him. "And I'll be happy to work with you as much as you want whenever you want."

"That would be great!" Tim said. "Maybe after class?"

"Uh, well," Lee stammered a bit. Right after class he was planning to ask Sensei if he could test. He'd waited long enough as it was. He couldn't put it off any longer. "I have something I need to do right after class today," Lee told Tim apologetically. "But any other time, honest."

"OK," Tim said.

"But I'll show you the block now," Lee said.

Lee checked their positions in the mirror. He and Tim both had their left fists in front of them and their right fists in the pocket. "Let's block with the other arm." Lee crossed his right arm in front of his left, making the X again. Then he blocked with his right arm and tucked his left fist back in the pocket.

Tim caught on a little quicker that time. After another few minutes, Tim actually seemed to be enjoying himself. That was one of the things Lee liked best about karate—taking raw, self-conscious white belts and molding them into deshi. Lee felt proud to be passing on such a great tradition, like the great karate masters of the past.

The familiar sound of a quiet footstep, though, instantly grabbed Lee's attention. Lee turned and saw Sensei Davis enter the deck from the curtained doorway of his office. A sturdy man in his late thirties, Sensei had straight sandy-colored hair with a bushy mustache to match.

"*Shotu-mate!*" Lee shouted loudly. That meant "Everybody stop what you're doing." As the most advanced student, it was Lee's responsibility to alert the other deshi whenever Sensei entered the room. Jeremy, Michael, and the other green belts stopped in the middle of their kata and stood up straight at attention. Rosalie stopped punching the makiwara, and Kevin stopped punching the air.

"*Sensei ni mawate!*" Lee yelled, telling everyone to turn towards Sensei. When everyone had obeyed, Lee shouted, "*Sensei ni rei!*" That was Japanese for "bow to Sensei."

"Onegai-shimasu, Sensei!" all the students cried, bowing towards Sensei. All the students, that is, except Tim, who just looked at Lee in confusion.

"Onegai-shimasu," Sensei Davis answered back. "*Shugo.* Line up."

"Don't worry," Lee whispered to Tim. "You'll get it. It just takes time." Then Lee took off at a jog towards the front of the class where Sensei stood by the shinden wall. They always formed two lines from the front of the dojo to the back with the most advanced student standing at the front of the left line. That was Lee's place.

Lee rushed forward past the white belts, the green belts, and the other brown belts to take his spot. He stood at attention, waiting for Sensei to give the command to bow. But Sensei said nothing. Sensei just stood there silently, facing the class.

Lee continued to stand in his place. He wondered why Sensei was taking so long to get started. Then

13

Lee became aware of something, a presence, some-where to his left. It was a quiet presence, a person breathing very softly. Lee was puzzled. Whoever it was wasn't standing in line like everyone else.

Lee turned his head slightly and swiveled his eyes. Nearby stood a girl he'd never seen before. She looked about twelve, and her thick dark hair was pulled back in a messy ponytail. She was wearing a karate uniform and looked straight ahead. She seemed to be waiting patiently. But waiting for what? Was she another new white belt who didn't know what was what?

Lee looked down at her belt and his eyes nearly popped out of his head. She wasn't a white belt. Not even close. This girl had a brown belt with black tips! This girl was more advanced than he was! Who was she? Where did she come from?

None of that mattered right now, Lee realized as he glanced back at Sensei who was also waiting pa-tiently. What did matter was that Lee was no longer standing in the right spot. He wasn't the most ad-vanced student anymore. This girl should take his place at the head of the class.

The way the class lined up, the most advanced student stood at the head of the first line, the one on the left. The second most advanced student stood at the head of the second line on the right. Then the other deshi arranged themselves left to right on down the lines in order of rank. By lining up in the wrong place, Lee made it so everyone had to move. Nothing like being upstaged in the most noticeable way possible, Lee thought grimly.

With a hasty bow to the girl, Lee stepped over to the front of the right line, taking Rosalie's place. Rosalie moved behind the new girl and other students shifted their spots down the lines back to Tim Unruh.

"*Kio-tsuke!*" Sensei shouted, calling them to attention.

"*Rei!*"

Everybody bowed to Sensei. "Onegai-shimasu, Sensei!"

"Onegai-shimasu," Sensei answered. "Sit, *seiza.*"

The new girl, Lee, and all the other deshi behind them sat in seiza position, their legs folded beneath them. Lee turned his palms up and cupped his hands on the knot of his belt.

"Close your eyes," Sensei said, "and empty your mind of all thought."

Usually, Lee loved this part of class where they meditated and calmed themselves so they could focus fully on karate. But today his mind wasn't calm at all. Today his whole mind was screaming one question: *Who was this new girl who'd taken his place?*

Chapter Two

Sensei clapped his hands loudly, breaking into Lee's thoughts.

Lee opened his eyes and stared straight ahead, willing himself to forget about the new girl. It was all he could do to keep from looking over at her, but he managed it.

Still in seiza position, Sensei turned towards the shinden wall. Now his back was towards the class, as they all faced the shinden wall together.

"Shinden ni rei," Sensei said, and everybody dropped their heads to the floor, bowing towards the photographs of the karate masters. This showed their respect for the teachers who'd come before them.

After a second or two, everybody raised their heads. Sensei turned back to face the class.

"*Dozo*," he said to the new girl, meaning "please." It was the responsibility of the highest ranking deshi to give the next command. It *used* to be Lee's responsibility.

"Sensei ni rei!" the new girl's voice rang out.

Everybody dropped their heads to the floor again, bowing to Sensei. "Onegai-shimasu, Sensei!" they shouted.

"Onegai-shimasu," Sensei said. "Everybody up."

Lee leapt right to his feet from seiza, a tricky move few deshi had the strength or balance to do. Lee was secretly pleased to see, out of the corner of his eye, that the new girl merely stood up like all the other deshi.

First Sensei led the class through some warm-up exercises. Then he directed half the class to form a line along the mirrored sidewall, facing inward. The other half of the class formed a second line and paired off with someone in the first line.

Lee found himself face to face with the new girl. She had a few freckles sprinkled across her nose and cheeks. Her wide-set green eyes were peaceful and calm. The expression in them reminded Lee of Sensei Davis.

"Kio-tsuke," Sensei called them to attention. "Rei."

The deshi bowed to their partners. Lee bowed to the new girl. "Onegai-shimasu, *sempai*," he said, adding "sempai" because she held a higher rank than he did. Sempai meant senior student.

"Onegai-shimasu," the girl said. Naturally, she didn't say "sempai" to Lee.

"We'll start with some techniques across the deck," Sensei said. "Wall side, you'll attack with a punch to the solar plexus. Defenders, you'll use a chest block. Attackers will keep punching, pushing your opponent to the opposite wall."

"*Arigato*, Sensei!" Lee and the other deshi shouted. *Arigato* meant thank you. You said thank you a lot in karate: after getting directions from an instructor, after being corrected, after working with an opponent. You could never be too polite or too respectful in karate.

"Right hand, right foot. Half speed," Sensei directed. "By the count. *Ichi!*" Sensei counted the number "one" in Japanese, and the attackers stepped forward on their right feet. Their right fists came forward in slow motion, aiming at the solar plexes of their opponents.

As the new girl's right fist slowly made its way towards the center of Lee's chest, he crossed his forearms in an X like the one he'd just shown Tim. Then Lee blocked with his left arm against the girl's punching arm, deflecting it from its target.

"*Ni!*" Sensei counted "two" in Japanese. The new girl stepped forward again, this time using her left foot and left fist. Again, Lee easily deflected her.

Lee hadn't realized how tense his body had been

until he felt it relax now as he backed across the floor. Sure, this girl had a higher rank than he did, but she was nothing to worry about. She was just another deshi. Rank wasn't so important, anyway. The color on your belt merely showed how many kata you'd learned so far.

When Lee and the rest of his line had reached the opposite wall, Sensei gave the command for them to reverse directions. "Ichi!" Sensei called, starting the count all over again.

Lee slowly threw his right fist towards the girl's solar plexus. Gently, she deflected it with her left arm, just as Lee had earlier. As Lee continued to step and punch, he noticed how slender she was. Her arms felt like toothpicks. It didn't matter what rank she held, Lee realized. If that poor kid ever got into a fight with someone bigger than she was, she'd had it. She'd snap like a twig.

When Lee and the new girl had punched and blocked back to the first wall, Sensei gave the next command. "With snap," he said, meaning using as much speed as they could. They still had to pull punches, though, which was a lot harder when you were also trying for speed. "No count," Sensei said. "*Hajime*." That was Japanese for "begin."

The new girl's right fist shot out so fast, Lee barely had time to block. Then her left fist was in his chest again, without Lee's having even seen it coming. Lee barely had time to make the X in front of his chest.

Something felt very wrong. No one could punch that fast unless they were cheating. That had to be it. The girl probably wasn't stepping first before punching, the way you were supposed to. She was probably throwing out her punches, *then* stepping.

Before the girl threw her next punch, Lee concentrated on her feet. He was trying to catch her in a mistake. Her foot moved forward, all right. Her fist came right after it, like a blur, landing squarely on Lee's solar plexus.

"Aaahh!" Lee gasped as he took the blow. His forearms had been nowhere near his chest that time. The pain in his solar plexus was so sharp he could barely breathe. Where did a skinny girl like that get so much power? Lee felt like he'd been hit with a cannonball.

The girl immediately dropped her fists. "I'm so sorry!" she apologized, touching Lee's arm. "I thought you were going to block. It's all my fault. I should've pulled back more. Are you OK?"

Lee nodded quickly, trying to act like it was nothing. Lee *was* supposed to block, but he hadn't. He'd been too busy looking at her feet. It was his own fault he'd been hit.

If Lee had been blocking the way he was supposed to, he would never have gotten hurt—whether his opponent forgot to pull punches or not. The girl probably felt sorry for Lee for being so dumb. That was why she was trying to make him feel better by saying it was her fault. Between the pain in his chest and the pity, Lee felt worse than ever.

"Are you all right?" the girl asked again. She looked worried.

"I'm fine," he said, glancing quickly over at Sensei. Sensei was looking right at them. Great. He'd seen the whole thing. "Let's keep going."

"Are you sure?" the girl asked.

Now some of the other deshi were looking at Lee, too. They were probably thinking what a wimp he was to let a simple exercise like that make him flinch. Lee had to prove them wrong. *"Let's keep going!"* Lee insisted, through gritted teeth.

"Arigato," the girl said. She threw another punch, but slower this time so Lee had plenty of time to block. Lee felt his face grow hot. She was treating him like a white belt. Still, even when she slowed down, this girl was unbeatable. She had a great sense of *ma-ai*, the space between herself and her opponent. She always placed herself at the perfect distance from Lee so she always had the advantage and he had the disadvantage.

She also had great *kime*, the ability to control and strengthen her blows for maximum impact. She kept her arms relaxed and loose as she threw out her punches, which gave her maximum speed. Then she tensed up at the split second of impact for maximum power. Lee had never seen such a natural fighter, male or female, adult or kid, in his entire life.

Lee wasn't jealous. Just the opposite. Lee was *glad* she'd come along. Aside from Sensei, Lee didn't have any other advanced deshi to watch and learn from. And that was the whole point of "onegai-shimasu," wasn't it? To learn and improve? This girl wasn't a threat. She was an opportunity.

When class was over, Sensei had them line up the way they'd done at the beginning of class. As Lee took his second-place spot, he smiled over at the girl, trying to make her feel welcome. She didn't see him. She was staring straight ahead, waiting for Sensei to give the command for them to sit.

"Sit, seiza," Sensei said. Lee closed his eyes and this time it was much easier to clear his mind. He felt at peace again. He'd conquered his negative feelings and filled himself with true karate spirit.

After bowing to the shinden and to Sensei, the class was dismissed. Lee was eager to ask Sensei for permission to test next week, but Sensei was still on the deck, talking to some of the other students. Lee would have to wait until Sensei was in his office.

Still filled with karate spirit, Lee looked around for Tim Unruh. Lee wasn't the most advanced student anymore, but it was still his responsibility to work with new white belts. If Lee could make Tim feel more confident, then Lee would have accomplished a great deal today.

Lee spotted Tim's blond head in the back of the classroom. Tim looked as confused as before. Smiling calmly, Lee headed across the wooden floor toward Tim.

"Onegai-shimasu," Lee said, bowing to Tim.

"Onegai-shimasu," Tim answered. Lee noticed that Tim was pronouncing the words better already.

"Would you like to work the first kata?" Lee asked the white belt. "I have some time to work with you, after all."

"Arigato," Tim said, bowing, "but somebody's already helping me."

Lee looked around. "Where?" he asked.

Tim pointed to a spot behind Lee. "Here she comes now," he said.

Lee turned and saw the new girl approach carrying two *chishi*. A chishi had a wooden handle with a metal weight stuck on one end. You held the end of the handle that didn't have the weight, and lifted and lowered the chishi to strengthen the muscles of your upper body.

"Onegai-shimasu," the new girl said, bowing. "Would you like to join us?" she asked Lee.

Lee looked from Tim to the new girl. Lee obviously wasn't needed here. Tim would get plenty of instruction without him. And Tim hadn't really chosen the new girl over him. Lee had made it very clear before class that he wouldn't be available to teach. So why did Lee have this funny feeling in the pit of his stomach?

"No, thanks," Lee said bowing. "Arigato, sempai."

"Arigato," the girl said.

Lee turned his back on the pair and headed for the men's locker room. His stomach was actually starting to gurgle now. Maybe he was just hungry. It *was* almost time for supper. Or maybe he was just nervous about asking Sensei for permission to test in the upcoming promotion.

That had to be it. Once he'd talked to Sensei he'd feel better. Even if Sensei said no, it would be better than the uncertainty of not knowing. But he hoped Sensei wouldn't say no.

Chapter Three

"Truly amazing," Michael was saying to Jeremy as Lee entered the locker room. Michael, his hair wet from the shower, was buttoning his shirt. Jeremy, a few feet away, was rinsing off his glasses in the sink.

"Awesome's more the word," Jeremy said, turning off the water and wiping his glasses dry with the tail of his cotton undershirt. "Did you see the way she snapped her hips on every move?" It was very important, in nearly every karate technique, to use your hips. A quick twisting movement of the hips was called a snap. Snapping the hips helped throw the full body weight into the technique, maximizing power and impact. "She's like a coiled spring," Jeremy raved on. "No wonder her punches had so much power."

Lee passed between his brothers and silently opened his locker. He knew they were talking about the new girl, but it didn't bother him. Every word they were saying was true. Lee had other things to think about right now. He wanted to take his shower as quickly as possible so he'd still have time to see Sensei.

"What do *you* think, Lee?" Michael asked as Lee stripped out of his sweaty gi and stepped into the shower stall.

Lee turned on the water full force so that it came pounding down on his chest and face. "About what?" Lee asked.

"About what? About *her!*" Michael exclaimed. "That's all anybody's been talking about since class ended. Have you ever seen anything like her in your life?"

"I can't hear you!" Lee said, starting to soap himself. Actually, he could sort of hear his brother, but it was hard to talk with the water running.

"The new girl!" Michael's voice was closer. He must have been standing right outside the shower stall. "What did you think of her?"

Lee was getting annoyed. Couldn't a guy take a shower in peace without someone shouting in his ear? Lee poked his head out from behind the plastic curtain. Michael and Jeremy were both standing a foot away, waiting for his answer. "I didn't think *anything*," Lee insisted. "She's just another student."

"Ha!" Jeremy said. "Then we're not talking about the same girl."

Lee sighed. It was obvious they weren't going to

stop talking to him until he said something. "She was good, OK?" he said, trying not to let his irritation show. "Now do you mind if I finish my shower?"

"Sorry," Michael said. "Is something wrong?"

Lee snapped off the faucets, grabbed his towel from the hook outside the stall, and dried himself off. "No," he said, walking past his brothers again and grabbing his clothes. "I'm just trying to get ready so I can talk to Sensei before we leave. There *is* a promotion coming up. Or have you forgotten? You were going to talk to Sensei too, remember?"

"Remember?" Jeremy crowed. "I've been looking forward to this all day!"

Lee pulled on his clothes, ran a comb through his hair, then stuffed his damp gi inside his blue knapsack. "So?" he asked his brothers. "What are we waiting for? Let's go!"

Lee slung his knapsack over his shoulder and charged out of the locker room, pausing for a fraction of a second to bow to the shinden wall. You had to bow to the shinden every time you entered or left the dojo. Michael and Jeremy followed close behind, also bowing. Then all three padded across the deck in their socks. Their shoes were stored in a closet by the front door of the dojo. Shoes weren't allowed on the deck.

When they reached the opposite side of the classroom, they bowed again and passed through another doorway leading to the front hall. The front wall had a long glass window so visitors could watch what was going on inside the classroom.

The other walls of the hall were covered with photographs of deshi past and present. Some of the photos showed deshi sparring or demonstrating techniques. Other photos were group portraits of deshi posing in uniform. Lee and his brothers were in some of those photographs. Sensei had one taken every year at their annual karate demonstration.

Lee started to head for the closet to get his shoes, but two people were standing in his way. They weren't just any two people. They were Sensei and the new girl. Lee stopped short, and his brothers bumped up behind him.

"What . . ." Jeremy started to say, but Lee shushed him. "Be quiet," he said. "We don't want to interrupt their conversation."

What Lee actually meant was that he wanted to *hear* their conversation. Lee was still very curious about who this new girl was, and he hoped to learn more by listening. The new girl was dressed, now, in a gray sweatshirt and faded blue jeans with holes in the knees. She still hadn't put her shoes on, so Lee could see that her sweatsocks had holes in them, too.

"So how *is* Sensei Modigliani?" Sensei Davis asked. "And how's his dojo doing?"

Well, that answered one question. The new girl had

studied with Sensei's former teacher, the one who had a dojo in North Carolina. This thought gave Lee some hope. Maybe the girl was just visiting. The Midvale Karate Dojo often had visitors from other dojo in the system.

"Sensei's fine," the new girl said in a soft voice. She had a slight southern accent. "I can't wait to see him next week when he comes up here for promotion. I really miss him."

"I miss him, too," Sensei Davis said. "He's a wonderful teacher. So how do you like your new school? Have you made many friends?"

So much for the "just visiting" theory. It looked like the new girl was here to stay.

"It's hard," the girl said, " 'cause we got here in the middle of the school year and a lot of people have their friends already. I'm not worried, though. I'm just happy my dad got transferred to a place that had a dojo in our system. That was a lucky break!"

Not all dojo used the same system of karate. There were many different styles with different kata and different ways of blocking, punching, and kicking. It would be hard to switch to a new dojo in a different system. Even if you'd earned your black belt in one style of karate, you'd have to start all over again as a white belt in a new system.

Sensei looked up and noticed Lee and his brothers standing in the doorway, listening. "Lee!" Sensei

29

called, waving the Jenkins boys over. "I'd like you to meet Jamie Oscarson. Her family just moved to Midvale."

Lee was embarrassed that Sensei had noticed him being nosy, but he tried not to show it. "Hi," Lee said, extending his hand to Jamie. "Nice to meet you." Michael and Jeremy shook her hand also.

"Well, I don't want to keep you," Jamie said to Sensei, "but I want to give you this before I go." She knelt and rummaged in her bookbag. She pulled out a square, flat package wrapped in brown paper and handed it to Sensei.

"Arigato," Sensei said, bowing. "Shall I open it?"

"Arigato, Sensei," Jamie said, bowing also.

Lee watched Sensei carefully peel back the Scotch tape on one of the brown paper flaps and slide a framed picture out of the wrapper. It was a watercolor painting of a samurai warrior. He wore a long kimono with an intricate pattern and held two swords, one short and one long.

"I made it to thank you," Jamie explained. "I'm so grateful to belong to your dojo now."

"*You* made this?" Sensei seemed surprised. "I'm impressed at your talent."

"Yeah," Michael echoed. "I wish I could paint like that." Michael was a good artist, too, but he concentrated his style on comic book illustration. That's what he wanted to do when he grew up.

30

Jamie blushed and bowed. "Arigato."

"I'll hang it in my office," Sensei said, tucking the painting and the wrapper under his arm. "I happen to have an empty space right above my desk. Arigato."

"Arigato, Sensei," Jamie said. "I'll see you tomorrow." Jamie turned towards the shoe closet and grabbed a pair of dirty gray sneakers.

Sensei smiled at Lee as he headed down the hall towards the door that led to his office. Jamie smiled at Lee, too, as she sat down on a low wooden bench by the closet and started to put on her sneakers.

Lee nodded at the girl. He would have liked to talk to her, to find out more about her and her training. He was especially curious to know how long she'd been studying to already have black tips on her belt. She didn't look any older than he was.

But Lee didn't have time right now. Sensei was in his office, all alone. This was Lee's chance to ask for permission to test. Lee turned towards his brothers. "I'll go first," he said. "Wish me luck."

Jeremy pounded his fist against the side of Lee's shoulder. Michael did the same. It was a new thing they'd figured out, like a secret signal, to wish each other luck. "See you in a few," Lee said, walking the last few feet to the doorway of Sensei's office.

Sensei was sitting behind his battered brown desk, studying the painting Jamie had just given him. Lee waited quietly in the doorway for Sensei to notice him. It would have been impolite to interrupt. To the right of Sensei's desk was a curtained doorway leading out into the karate classroom.

Sensei looked up. His dark brown eyes glowed like shiny buttons. "Come in, Lee," he said, moving the painting to the side of his desk. "Sit down."

Lee took a seat on the straight-backed wooden chair facing Sensei. Above Sensei's desk were framed certificates tracing the history of his promotions in the karate system. The first one recorded the day, fifteen years ago, when Sensei had earned his first green tip. The last certificate, a few years old, announced Sensei's promotion to third-degree black belt.

There were ten degrees of black belt altogether. Only Master Nagamine, the founder of their style of karate back in Okinawa, had a tenth-degree black belt. Master Ueshiro, the man who'd brought the style to the United States, had an eighth-degree black belt. Sensei Modigliani, Sensei Davis's teacher from North Carolina, had a fifth-degree black belt.

Sensei leaned back in his upholstered chair and waited for Lee to speak.

Lee's heart began to pound hard. His chest felt tight, and his palms were sweaty. Now that the moment had arrived, it was hard to get up the nerve to ask the big question. But Lee couldn't just sit there staring at Sensei.

"Onegai-shimasu, Sensei," Lee began respectfully. "I was, uh, wondering . . . I mean, what I would like to do is ask for permission . . . I mean, if you thought I was ready, I would like to test for black tips, but, uh, what do you think?"

You idiot! Lee chided himself. He'd only used about ten times as many words as he needed to ask a simple question. If Sensei *had* been willing to give him permission before, he probably wouldn't now that Lee had made such a total fool of himself.

Sensei stroked his sandy mustache with the tip of his index finger. "You'd like to test," he said, nodding. "I see. Let's review your record."

Lee sat up straight, waiting for Sensei to question him. This was what had happened all the other times Lee had asked for permission to test. And all the other times, Sensei had said yes. Maybe this was a good sign.

"How long have you been at the dojo?" Sensei asked.

"Five years," Lee said. His voice squeaked a little on the last word.

"And how long at your present rank of brown belt?" Sensei asked.

Lee cleared his throat. "Two years," he said. Even though these were just simple questions, he was finding it difficult to remember the answers. His head was spinning.

33

"And how often do you train?" Sensei asked. "On average."

"I come about four times a week," Lee said.

Sensei nodded. Nothing in his face made it look like he was going to turn Lee down, but Lee didn't see anything encouraging there, either.

"And what have you done to help the dojo?" Sensei asked. "As I'm sure you know by now, showing good spirit is the most important part of your training."

"Arigato, Sensei," Lee said, bowing his head. "Well, I work with white-belt students whenever I can, and I've organized several clean-ups of the locker room when I noticed it was messy."

Sensei nodded. "Anything else?"

Lee thought hard. He'd done a lot for the dojo, more than any other kid that he knew, but it was hard to think right now. "I baked cookies for the dojo holiday party last year, and sometimes I sweep the sidewalk in front of the dojo," Lee added. The dojo was located in the Midvale Mall, between Vinnie's Pizzeria and Plaza Shoes.

"Is that all?" Sensei asked. His voice was neutral.

Lee nodded. He suddenly felt guilty, as if he hadn't done enough. Maybe Sensei thought so, too. Maybe that would stand in the way of Lee getting permission to test. After all, this was the last rank before black belt. The higher you went, the tougher the requirements.

Sensei appeared to be deep in thought. What was taking him so long to make up his mind? Was Lee a borderline case? Lee tried not to look at Sensei so he wouldn't seem so eager. Lee focused, instead, on Jamie's watercolor.

Then Lee understood. Compared to someone like Jamie, who already had her black tips, Lee must have looked pretty shabby. No wonder Sensei wasn't saying yes.

"You have permission," Sensei said.

Lee's head jerked up. He wasn't sure he'd heard correctly. But Sensei gazed at him steadily with his dark brown eyes, a small smile on his face.

"I do?" Lee shouted, instantly regretting how undignified he sounded. This was a moment when Lee was supposed to be showing his maturity, and instead he was acting like an excited little kid. Lee forced himself to rise slowly to his feet. Then he bowed low. "Arigato, Sensei," he said.

"Arigato," Sensei Davis said.

It took every ounce of strength Lee had to make himself walk calmly out of the room, as befitted a soon-to-be brown belt with black tips. But as soon as he got outside to where his brothers were waiting, safely out of Sensei's range of vision, Lee began to jump up and down.

"He said yes!" Lee said, waving his fists in the air. "Sensei said yes!"

Chapter Four

"Of *course* he said yes," Jeremy told Lee, slapping his brother on the back. "What did you *think* he'd say?"

Lee shrugged. "I don't know. I really thought it could go either way."

Jeremy rolled his eyes. He could never understand how Lee could be so modest. Lee was the best karate student in the whole dojo—at least, he had been until that girl Jamie showed up. But Jamie or no Jamie, Lee was more than ready to test for black tips.

"I guess I'm next," Michael said, biting his lower lip. He glanced towards the door to Sensei's office, but he didn't move.

"What are you waiting for?" Jeremy asked his oldest brother, giving him the good luck punch. "Go in there!"

Michael hesitated. "I don't know. Maybe I should wait until the next promotion."

What was with his brothers? Jeremy wondered. Sure it was a little scary facing up to Sensei and putting yourself on the line. There was no point being bashful about it, though. You had to be bold. Jump right in. That's what Jeremy always did.

Jeremy gave Michael a little push. "You're ready *now*," Jeremy insisted. "Just go and get it over with. It won't take long." *And the sooner you're done, the sooner I can go in and get permission for myself,* Jeremy thought to himself.

Jeremy could already picture himself with brown tips on his green belt. Those brown tips meant he could learn three more kata and the third prearranged fighting sequence. Brown tips meant he could stand further up in the line when they started and ended class. And anyone green belt or lower would have to bow to him and call him sempai. Having brown tips was going to be great.

Michael took a few tentative steps towards Sensei's door. "Wish me luck," he said. His face looked pale, like he was sick or something.

Jeremy pounded Michael on the shoulder again, and this time Lee did the same.

After Michael had disappeared into Sensei's office, Lee began to pace up and down the narrow hall. "Black tips," he murmured disbelievingly. "I can't believe it. I've been waiting for this for so long . . ."

"Did I hear someone say tips?" asked Jon Walker,

a boy with light brown hair, stepping through the doorway from the classroom. Jon was a green belt, just like Jeremy. They'd tested together at the last promotion and they'd started at the dojo around the same time.

"Lee's testing for black tips," Jeremy volunteered since Lee was still in too much of a daze to talk.

"That's great," Jon said. "I'm testing, too, for brown tips. Sensei gave me permission right before class."

"Cool," Jeremy said. "When I get *my* brown tips, we can be training partners." Training partners were deshi of the same rank who practiced together.

"Cool," Jon echoed, pulling a pair of scuffed loafers out of the shoe closet. He dropped them on the floor and stepped into them. "See you tomorrow."

As Jon pushed through the glass door to leave the dojo, Michael came out of Sensei's office, a huge smile on his face.

"Let me guess," Jeremy said. "He said yes."

Michael simply nodded, then went to sit on the wooden bench. "I just hope I don't choke at the promotion," he said, shaking his head. "I hope I don't forget all my katas." Michael was a bit of a worrier.

"Don't think negative," Jeremy said. "You've been doing this for years already."

Lee banged his fist against Jeremy's shoulder. "Your turn," he said.

Jeremy took a deep breath. There was nothing to be afraid of. Asking for permission was probably just a formality anyway. Sensei had said yes to everyone else. "See you in a minute," Jeremy said, giving his brothers the thumbs-up.

Jeremy strode to Sensei's open door and knocked on the doorjamb. Sensei, still in his uniform, sat behind his desk writing something on a clipboard.

Jeremy waited until Sensei looked up, then he bowed deeply. "Onegai-shimasu, Sensei," he said in a loud, booming voice. Jeremy had practiced this in his mind a thousand times, so he knew exactly what to say and do. He had to show spirit and respect and use all the proper terms of courtesy.

"Onegai-shimasu," Sensei said. "Would you like to sit down?"

Of course I would! Jeremy answered silently. *Why do you think I'm here?* But, of course, Jeremy didn't say that. That would have been rude. "Arigato, Sensei," Jeremy said, bowing again. Then he marched to the wooden chair and sat down. He placed his hands on his knees and sat with a very straight back, eyes straight ahead. Jeremy was sure he looked like a fierce warrior.

"What can I do for you, Jeremy?" Sensei asked.

"I would like permission to test for brown tips," Jeremy said, barking the words like a soldier.

Sensei's dark brown eyes gazed back at Jeremy with their usual, peaceful expressionless gaze. "I see," he said. "How long have you been at the dojo?"

"Three and a half years, Sensei," Jeremy said.

"And how long have you held your present rank of green belt?"

"Six months, Sensei," Jeremy said.

"How often do you train?" Sensei asked.

Jeremy was getting impatient. Sensei knew the answers to all these questions. Sensei kept attendance records for all his students. But of course Jeremy couldn't let his impatience show. He had to answer every question no matter how he felt. "Three or four times a week, Sensei!" he shouted.

"No need to yell," Sensei said, fiddling with his ear, "though I appreciate the spirit."

"Sorry, Sensei," Jeremy said, lowering his voice.

Sensei crossed his hands on his desk and leaned forward. Jeremy looked into Sensei's calm dark eyes. This was it. This was the part where Sensei said yes. Jeremy had seen this in his mind a thousand times, too.

"Your attendance is good, Jeremy," Sensei said. "And you've made tremendous progress since you started."

Jeremy nodded happily. Sensei wasn't telling him anything he didn't already know.

Sensei reached into his drawer and pulled out an

index card and a pen. Jeremy wasn't quite sure how this fit into the permission process. Was Jeremy supposed to fill out a card or sign his name or something?

Sensei wrote down something on the card and handed it to Jeremy, along with a clear plastic pushpin that he also pulled from the drawer. "Before you leave the dojo," he said, "I'd like you to put this up on the bulletin board."

Jeremy was confused. He read the card. It said:

Patience is the essential quality of a man.
　　　　　　　　　　—Kwai-Koo-Tsu

After he'd read the card, Jeremy felt even more confused.

"I don't understand," Jeremy said.

Sensei was quiet for a moment. Then he said, "Despite your progress, I don't think you're ready to test yet for the next level. You've really just started learning the first two Pinan katas, and they still need a lot of work. I'd also like you keep working on your basic techniques."

Basic techniques? Sensei was talking as though Jeremy was still a white belt who didn't know how to do a simple chest block, not a guy who was ready to move into the advanced ranks. And what about Jon Walker? He been studying karate for exactly the same amount of time as Jeremy, and *he'd* been allowed to test. Jeremy had never known Sensei to play favorites, but that was sure the way it looked right now.

Jeremy felt his eyes smart with tears. This was so unfair! But Jeremy couldn't say anything to Sensei or Sensei would think he was being disrespectful. Then Sensei would *never* let him test.

Jeremy blinked rapidly until his eyes were clear. Then he stood up stiffly and bowed. "Arigato, Sensei," he said. His voice sounded wobbly, but he couldn't help it.

"Arigato. Don't forget the card," Sensei said.

Jeremy took the card and thumbtack off Sensei's desk. Barely glancing at it, he quickly left Sensei's office.

Lee and Michael were waiting outside Sensei's door. "Well?" they asked, their faces filled with the happiness of their own success.

Jeremy merely shook his head then pushed past them, reentering the classroom. The bulletin board was right inside the door. Sensei was always putting up different quotes on the board, bits of wisdom from the ancient masters that students were supposed to read and think about. But Jeremy didn't want to think about anything right now. Finding an empty space on the brown corkboard, he jabbed the thumbtack into the new index card. Then, barely bowing to the shinden, he left the deck again and headed for the shoe closet.

"Jeremy," Lee said, reaching for his arm. "What happened?"

"I don't want to talk about it," Jeremy said. He grabbed his sneakers from the shoe closet and stuffed his feet into them. Then, without bothering to tie them, he pushed open the door and headed outside for the bicycle rack.

Michael rushed after him. "Jeremy!" he called, following Jeremy out the door. "What did Sensei say?"

Jeremy didn't answer. He fumbled in his pocket for the key to his bicycle lock. It had gotten lost among the coins, paper clips, rubber bands, yo-yo, and pencil stubs that he always kept on hand. As he fumbled, he felt his face grow hot. His brothers were waiting patiently, but that didn't make Jeremy feel any better. He was having a really bad day.

Meanwhile, across the mall parking lot, there was Jon Walker getting into his mother's car. They were both laughing and smiling. Well, they had something to feel good about. Jeremy was sure Jon had just told her about getting permission to test.

This day had turned into a real nightmare. And it was all Sensei's fault. How could Sensei have given Jon permission and not Jeremy? Could Sensei really believe Jeremy wasn't ready yet? Was Sensei suddenly blind or something?

Jeremy was more than ready. He was strong, he

was fast, and he knew all the kata he was supposed to. There had to be a way to make Sensei see this, to make Sensei change his mind.

That was it! Sensei was a reasonable man. All Jeremy had to do was prove he was ready. Jeremy was sure he could do this somehow. Sensei would give him permission to test after all. He'd have to. The only problem was: Jeremy didn't have any idea how to prove himself. Yet.

Bingo! Jeremy felt his key nestled in a wad of lint and rubber bands way down in his pocket. It was like a sign, he thought. As soon as he began to think positively, he found his key. His luck was changing. He would find a way to convince Sensei. Jeremy was sure of it.

With a whoop, he pushed off on his bicycle. He pedaled furiously, as if he could pedal away all the frustrations of the past half hour. He didn't even pay attention to his two brothers as they struggled to catch up.

The cool breeze felt good against Lee's face as he stepped outside the sixth-grade wing, Tuesday after school. The school building had felt stuffier than usual, or maybe it was just that Lee had felt so restless all day. He couldn't wait to get back to the dojo and practice all his katas for the promotion Sunday.

He had his chance now, though. Lee headed for

the bicycle rack where he always met Michael and Jeremy after school. Neither one of them was there yet.

"Lee?"

Lee turned around and saw Jamie Oscarson coming out of the sixth-grade wing. She was wearing the same dirty, ripped jeans she'd worn the day before with a different sweatshirt.

"Hi, Jamie," Lee said, trying to sound friendly. He still wasn't too crazy about the girl, but there was no need to be rude. In fact, he *couldn't* be rude, even if he wanted to. She was his sempai, a senior student, so he had to show respect whether they were in the dojo or not.

"You going to karate?" Jamie asked.

Lee nodded. "But I have to wait for my brothers."

"Oh." Jamie started unlocking her bike. Lee got the feeling that she was purposely taking her time, maybe because she wanted to talk or something. Lee remembered that Jamie had said it was hard making friends in Midvale. Well, Lee had a few minutes.

"How long have you been in Midvale?" Lee asked.

Jamie stopped fiddling and smiled at Lee. "A little over a week," she told him. "We moved in the weekend before last. I would have gone to the dojo sooner, but my parents made me do all this other stuff after school last week like unpack boxes and set up my room."

45

Lee shrugged. "Well, I guess you've got to do what you've got to do. So, you used to study with Sensei Modigliani, Sensei Davis's old teacher? What's he like?"

Jamie's wide-set eyes grew dreamy. "He's wonderful," she said. "To look at him, you'd never guess he's such a powerful fighter, 'cause he's skinny and he acts so quiet. But he's incredibly fast and his techniques are almost perfect. I used to watch him spar with Sempai Hall, this first-degree black belt from my old dojo. Sempai Hall was, like, six feet five, two hundred and fifty pounds, but Sensei Modigliani used to beat him every time. It was amazing!"

"You don't have to be taller or heavier than your opponent to win," Lee agreed. "Good technique counts for a lot."

"That's what Sensei Modigliani always says," Jamie agreed. She stood up and knocked over the pink bookbag she'd placed on the ground by her bike. Lee saw a pile of textbooks slide out, along with some messy papers, spiral notebooks with doodles all over them, and a dog-eared copy of *The Book of Five Rings*.

Lee recognized the book right away. It was his favorite book in the entire world. *The Book of Five Rings* was written by Miyamoto Musashi, the greatest samurai warrior who'd ever lived. Musashi was also Lee's personal hero. Born in the 1500s, Musashi became a master of kendo, the art of the sword. By the time he was thirty years old, Musashi had fought and won more than sixty contests. This was a very great achievement for such a young master. Musashi then went to live in a cave in the mountains of Japan. That was where he wrote *The Book of Five Rings,* which explains his winning strategies.

Lee had read the book at least fifty times, and every time he read it he found something new. Musashi's strategies weren't just useful for fighting physical battles. You could use them to deal with anyone who was giving you a hard time. Lee's copy of Musashi's book was in a lot better shape than Jamie's, though. Lee kept his on a shelf at home and always made sure his hands were clean before he read it. Jamie's copy, on the other hand, was now lying in the dusty dirt next to the sidewalk.

"Uh, your Musashi's getting dirty," Lee said. *Even dirtier* was what he really meant. How could Jamie treat the book with so little respect? Not that it was so surprising when you looked at the rest of her. Her hair was messy and her sneakers were dirty and her pants were always ripped. It just didn't seem like good karate spirit to be such a slob.

"Hmmm?" Jamie asked. She was busy trying to untangle her bicycle, which had gotten hooked into two other bicycles.

"Your books," Lee repeated. "They're all over the ground."

Jamie ripped her bicycle away from the others, scraping off some of the yellow paint on its frame. Then she looked down and noticed what Lee had been talking about. "Oh!" she exclaimed. She dropped her bicycle with a crash and stooped down beside the pile of books.

"You like Musashi?" Lee asked.

"*Like* him?" Jamie exclaimed as she picked up the tattered volume. "He's only my favorite hero who ever lived. I must have read his book at least fifty times."

Lee knew he should have been happy that someone else admired Musashi as much as he did. But for some reason, he felt annoyed.

"I'm trying to model my whole life after Musashi," Jamie said. "I want to perfect myself the way he did, and I want to be a great warrior and a great artist, just like him."

Come to think of it, the watercolor that Jamie had given Sensei yesterday sort of looked like the paintings Lee had seen in Musashi's book. Musashi had not only been a master of the sword, but also a master of many arts, especially ink painting. Lee remembered reading that Musashi hadn't cared much about his appearance, either. It was said that he never brushed his hair. He never took a bath, either, for fear of being caught without his weapon.

Lee was beginning to feel a strong urge to get away

from Jamie. He looked around for his brothers. There was still no sign of Michael or Jeremy, but they probably wouldn't care that much if Lee went to the dojo without them.

"I want to open my own dojo, too, when I grow up," Jamie volunteered. "I want to be a Sensei."

Lee was starting to get that funny feeling in his stomach again. He was sorry he'd spoken to her in the first place.

It seemed that no matter what Lee did, this Jamie got there ahead of him. She even wanted to do the same things he did. And she'd probably be better at all of them, he thought bitterly, like she was now.

Relax and breathe, a voice in Lee's head reminded him, echoing Sensei Davis. *Don't let her upset you. This is no different from the situations Musashi wrote about in his book. Jamie may not be carrying swords, but she's still an opponent. Don't let her psych you out just because you think she's better than you.*

Lee tried to empty his mind so he could think clearly and find his opponent's weakness. Was Jamie really better than he was? Not necessarily. She was just more advanced. That simply meant that Jamie had been doing karate *longer* than he had. Once Lee had as much training as she did, he could be just as good as she was—if not better. Which brought up a major question. How long had Jamie been studying karate, anyway?

"By the way," Lee said, trying to sound offhand, "how long have you been training?"

Jamie carelessly scooped up all her stuff and jammed it back into her bookbag. "Four years," she said, picking up her bicycle and tossing her bookbag in the wire basket in front of the handlebars.

Four years? Lee had been studying for five! Jamie didn't even realize it, but she'd just defeated him as completely as if she'd run him through with a sword.

"I've got to go," Lee said, trying not to let his misery show in his face or voice. He quickly unlocked his bicycle and threw the chain in his knapsack. "If you see my brothers, will you tell them I went to the dojo?"

"OK." Jamie started to say something else, but she was drowned out by the whoops and yells of four boys who coasted, two to a bike, down the hill next to the school. They turned in at the entrance behind the sixth-grade wing and skipped to a stop right in front of Lee and Jamie.

Lee had never seen any of them before. They looked a little older than he was, maybe thirteen or fourteen. They were bigger, too, and beefier. The biggest one of all, a guy with a shaved head and a gold skull earring in one ear, hopped off one of the bicycles and approached Lee.

"Nice bike," he said, looking down at Lee's shiny red ten-speed. He was smiling, but his eyes were cold. Lee had a very bad feeling about this guy. He hadn't stopped by just to admire Lee's bike. Lee also knew it would be a mistake to show fear.

"Thanks," Lee said, staring coolly into the guy's eyes.

Skull, the guy with the skull earring, let his hand rest lightly on Lee's handlebars. "Mind if I take it for a test drive?" he asked.

Lee knew that if this guy rode off with his bike, it would be the last time Lee ever saw it. "Sorry," Lee said. "No can do."

Skull grinned nastily. His big dirty hands clamped onto Lee's handlebars. "I'm disappointed in you," he said as his friends moved in behind him. "Don't you believe in sharing?" He turned to his buddies and sneered, "Get a load of Mr. Selfish here."

The other guys started snickering. "Hey, Skull," one of them said back, "maybe we should teach him some manners, huh?"

Skull pushed the bike towards one of his friends. Now there was nothing between him and Lee. Then he took a step closer so that he and Lee were face to face. "Good idea," he said.

Chapter Five

Skull's nose was just an inch away. Lee was dying to give the guy a headbutt. He imagined jerking his head forward and breaking the guy's nose with his forehead. The guy wouldn't be expecting it, and Lee knew his technique would be effective.

Lee couldn't go through with it, of course. *Karate ni sente nashi*. There was no first attack in karate. Someone *threatening* to attack you didn't count. The only way you could strike was if the opponent made the first move.

Lee was ready, though. The adrenaline was pumping through his veins, filling his body with raw energy. His heart was pounding so hard Lee felt like his whole body was beating. Out of the corner of his eye, Lee noticed that Jamie had moved closer to him on his left side.

"Last chance, buddy boy," Skull said. "You can give it to me nice and easy. Or I can take it from you and I promise it won't be nice. Either way, it's mine.

"Hey!" a man's voice called from off to Lee's right. "What's going on over there?"

Lee knew that voice. Most of the time when he heard it, he dreaded it because it was the voice of Mr. Cefari, the vice principal. Mr. Cefari was always rooting around for trouble and yelling at you whether you deserved it or not. But today Lee was happy that Mr. Cefari had found him.

Skull took a half-step back, but he put his hand on Lee's bike. One of his buddies had been holding onto it while Skull menaced Lee. Now he pushed it back toward Skull.

"Huh?" Skull said, making himself sound stupid. "I don't know what you're talking about."

"Don't give me that," Mr. Cefari said, charging forward. He wasn't very tall, maybe five foot five. He was nearly bald, with a fringe of dark brown hair wrapping around his head from ear to ear. Still, most people were afraid of him and with good reason. "I know what you're doing here," Mr. Cefari said, stepping right up to Skull, who was several inches taller. "And I'm tired of seeing you punks hanging around this school."

"It's a free country," said one of the other boys. He wore a denim jacket with a bloody dagger embroidered on the back. "We can go wherever we want."

Mr. Cefari turned to Bloody Dagger. "Oh yeah?

53

Then maybe you've never heard the word *trespass-ing*. You're not students here. You don't belong here. So get lost!"

"Hey, I'm a student," one boy said. "You don't know nothing."

Mr. Cefari sneered. "I know every single person who goes to this school, and I know you're not one of them. I also happen to know you go to Weston Junior High. I know your principal, and I know all your names."

Skull turned to his friends. Suddenly his face didn't look so tough. In fact, he looked worried. "Maybe we'd better get out of here," he said.

"Good answer!" Mr. Cefari said, applauding. "I'll give you"—he checked his watch—"oh, let's say three seconds."

"Or what?" Skull challenged.

Mr. Cefari's eyes took on an evil gleam. "Three . . ." he counted backward, "two . . ."

Skull let go of Lee's bike. Without a word, he hopped on one of the bicycles they'd arrived on. The other boys followed and, two to a bike, they rode quickly away.

Lee didn't realize he'd been holding his breath until he took a huge gulp of air. "Thanks, Mr. Cefari," he said.

"My pleasure," Mr. Cefari said grimly. Then he

looked at Lee and Jamie. "You kids stay out of trouble," he said gruffly.

Without another word, the vice principal opened
the back door to the sixth-grade wing and disappeared
inside.

Lee's heart was still pounding as he straddled his
bike. He was grateful that Mr. Cefari had saved them,
but he also felt a little disappointed. All that adrenaline pumping through his veins had nowhere to go.
Lee felt like punching a hole through the brick wall
of the sixth-grade wing.

Jamie, on the other hand, seemed absolutely un-
affected by what had just happened. Her eyes were
calm and her face showed no sign of fear or relief.

"I don't get it," Lee said. "You're so calm about
this. Those guys might have stolen your bike, too.
Weren't you afraid?"

"Sure I was," Jamie said. "But remember what
Masoyama said. 'The karateist is a tranquil person. He
is unafraid. He can be calm in a burning building.' "

Easy for you to say, Lee thought to himself. Sure,
he'd read all the same quotes Jamie had but he had
to work very hard at making all that karate wisdom
part of his life. Jamie, on the other hand, didn't seem
to have to work at it at all. Everything seemed to
come so naturally to her. No wonder she was ahead
of him.

"Sorry we're late," Michael said, coming down the walk with Jeremy. "The advisor for the school paper stopped me in the hall 'cause she wants me to do a cartoon for the next issue."

"And my science teacher wanted me to show him how I figured out that bonus question on my test," Jeremy added. "He made me write it down so he can show it to everybody."

Lee shrugged. "No problem. I just don't want to be late for class. Let's go."

Jamie cleared her throat, then looked down at the ground. "Uh, I don't want to be pushy or anything," she said, "but could I ride to the dojo with you guys? I sort of got lost yesterday when I rode my bike from school."

Lee looked from Michael to Jeremy, hoping one of them would say no. It wasn't that he didn't like Jamie, but he'd already spent more time with her than he'd wanted to today.

"Sure you can come with us, sempai," Michael said good-naturedly. "Those back roads are tricky until you get to know them." He unlocked his bicycle and wheeled it beside Lee's.

"I'll show you how to get there if you'll help me work on my kata," Jeremy said, grinning at Jamie. "It would be an honor to work with a sempai like you."

Lee couldn't believe it. Had his brothers really turned on him this quickly? Didn't they know how bad it made him feel the way they were kissing up to her? Michael was treating her like she was Sensei Davis! Even Jeremy was pouring on the charm. Ever since a recent comic book convention, girl-hating Jeremy had completely changed.

They all hopped on their bicycles and coasted down the hill towards the mall where the dojo was. Within minutes, they were cutting across the huge parking lot, dodging parked cars and shoppers. The Midvale Mall had eighty-seven stores and a twelve-plex movie theater. A long covered walkway ran along the front of the stores. Lee, his brothers, and Jamie pulled up in front of the dojo and locked their bicycles.

"I know there's not much time before class," Jeremy told Jamie as they pushed open the front door, "but promise me we can work together afterwards?"

"Sure," Jamie said, kicking off her sneakers and tossing them in the shoe closet.

"Hey, look," Michael said, pointing through the open doorway to Sensei's office. Jamie's watercolor now hung prominently over Sensei's desk. "You're a really good painter," Michael told Jamie. "Have you taken any art classes?"

"Some," Jamie said, "back in North Carolina."

"Where?" Michael asked.

Jamie looked down. "Well, actually, I won a full summer scholarship to the State Academy of Fine Arts three years in a row. Fortunately, it was near where we lived so I didn't have to give up my karate training."

As Lee looked from Michael's admiring face to Jeremy's, he started to feel more and more depressed. It used to be that Lee was the one who couldn't wait to get to the dojo every day. Now that Jamie was around, Lee almost wished he could be anyplace else.

"Shugo, line up for kata on the wooden deck," Sensei Davis said a little later after the class had finished warm-ups. "Rank order."

Jeremy, who'd been standing in the front part of the classroom which was covered with a padded mat, ran at breakneck speed towards the back of the classroom to take his proper place in line. Class had only started a few minutes before, but his body was already dripping with sweat. His gi looked like he'd taken a shower in it.

That was exactly the way Jeremy wanted it. Jeremy had only five days left to prove to Sensei that he was ready to test. In order to do that, Jeremy knew he had to try harder and show more spirit than anyone else. Jeremy took his place in the middle of the left line. Jon Walker stood next to him in the middle of the right line. Perfect. With Jon right next to him, Jeremy could prove to Sensei that he was at least as good as Jon, if not better.

"*Fukyugata Ichi,*" Sensei said. "First kata. Light snap. *Yo-i!*"

That was the command to take the "ready" position. Jeremy's feet were already in place, heels together, toes pointing outward at an angle. Now Jeremy crossed his flattened palms over his groin.

"Ichi!" Sensei counted one.

Jeremy and the rest of the class dropped low and covered their ribs, protecting themselves from an imaginary opponent who was kicking them from the left. Then Jeremy stepped to the left and did a downward strike with his left arm against the imaginary kick. This was called a down block.

Fukyugata Ichi was the most basic kata and the first one any deshi learned when he or she joined the dojo. It was made up of twenty-one choreographed moves, mostly down blocks, high blocks, and walking punches.

Twenty-one moves might seem like a lot, but Jeremy had been practicing this first kata for ages. He couldn't even count how many times he'd done it. Enough to make it seem old to Jeremy—real old. Still, no way could he afford to act as bored as he felt. He was going to do every move like his life depended on it.

"Ni!" Sensei counted two. Jeremy stomped forward on his right foot and rammed his right fist into his imaginary opponent's solar plexus.

"Ichi!" Sensei called, counting one to mark the beginning of the next movement in the kata. Jeremy stepped back with his right foot and whirled around with a right down block to the other side, fighting off a second imaginary opponent. In all the kata, you imagined that you were surrounded by attackers. You had to make sure you neutralized each opponent before moving on to the next.

"Ni!"

Jeremy shot his left fist forward with such force that he nearly knocked himself off balance.

"Ichi!"

As Jeremy moved into the next down block, he sneaked a look at Jon Walker. Jon wasn't trying anywhere near hard as Jeremy was. He looked OK. He just wasn't putting as much *spirit* into it as Jeremy was.

Then Jeremy glanced towards Sensei to see if he noticed all this. Sensei wasn't even looking in Jeremy's direction.

Jeremy wasn't going to give up. As he moved into the next series of moves, three walking punches, Jeremy pretended he was a battering ram breaking through a brick wall. His gi snapped like a flag in high wind each time he threw out his fist. Jeremy's punches had never had so much power.

Jeremy looked over at Sensei again. Now he was

working with Kevin Whittaker, straightening out his fist. Kevin had it bent too far back. His knuckles were pointing up instead of straight ahead at his target, like they were supposed to.

On the next count, Jeremy and the others snapped around in another down block, followed by a high block to protect against an imaginary punch to the face. They repeated the down block and high block on the other foot.

The next move would really be Jeremy's chance to shine. It was the kiai move, the one where they all shouted as loud as they could to startle their opponents.

"*Hyaaaaaaaaaaaaah!*" Jeremy shouted, longer and louder than anybody else, as they all lunged forward on their left feet and threw reverse punches with their right fists.

Sensei walked right past Jeremy. He stopped in front of Jon Walker. Jeremy held his breath. What was Sensei up to now? All Sensei did was reach over and tuck Jon's left fist further back in the pocket. Jeremy let out his breath.

Jeremy wished he could shout again, even though the kiai move was already over. What more did he have to do to get Sensei's attention? Sensei seemed to be purposely ignoring him.

Suddenly, Jeremy understood. Sensei *was* ignoring

him, and Jeremy knew why. Sensei was probably still mad at Jeremy for messing up at the outdoor karate demonstration last month.

Jeremy had been demonstrating *Pinan Shodan*, the first green-belt kata. His brothers and Dwight Vernon were doing *bunkai,* which meant that they were being Jeremy's real opponents instead of Jeremy fighting imaginary ones. Hundreds of people had been watching, along with a local TV news camera.

Things had been going great until Jeremy had slipped on the stage and fallen on his butt. Everyone had laughed and Jeremy had run off the stage. It was the most humiliating day of his life.

Jeremy had talked to Sensei about it afterwards. Sensei had *said* he wasn't angry, but Jeremy knew better, now. Of course Sensei was upset. Jeremy had made the whole school look bad by his poor performance. And now Sensei was paying him back.

Jeremy had to find a way to make it up to Sensei, to prove he'd learned from his mistakes so Sensei would forgive him. Maybe Jamie could give him some ideas about how to do this, or maybe he could talk to Lee after class. One way or another, Jeremy had to change Sensei's mind.

After they'd practiced Fukyugata Ichi over and over again, Sensei gave the command to "split the deck." Lee backed up quickly against the side wall, joining a line of other deshi. The other half of the class lined up against the opposite wall.

"Two volunteers," Sensei requested.

Lee raced to the center of the deck, getting there a fraction of a second after Jamie Oscarson but beating his brother, Jeremy. Lee was a little surprised to see Jeremy so enthusiastic today. He'd been punching and kicking and kiaiing like a maniac. Instead of being depressed that Sensei had turned him down for promotion, Jeremy seemed to be acting like Super Deshi.

"Lee and Jamie, stay up," Sensei said.

Reluctantly, Jeremy backed towards the line he'd come from.

"Today we're going to practice *jyu-kumite,* or sparring," Sensei said. "Is there anyone here who's never done it before?"

Timothy Unruh, the brand-new white belt, shyly raised his hand.

"Arigato," Sensei said. "Our brown belt volunteers will demonstrate. Sparring is your chance to take the techniques you've learned in your kata and apply them to a more freestyle situation. When you get out on the street, you're not going to know exactly what move your opponent is going to do, the way we do in kata or prearranged fighting. You have to be able to call upon your techniques without thinking about them."

"Arigato, Sensei!" Jeremy shouted at the top of his lungs.

In certain situations, all the deshi said arigato together. But you could also shout arigato at other times, by yourself, to show you'd understood a correction or piece of advice. This showed your spirit and willingness to learn. Lee thought Jeremy was going a little overboard today, though. It seemed like he was trying too hard to impress Sensei.

"Kio-tsuke!" Sensei called them to attention.

Lee and Jamie turned to face each other, heels together, toes turned out.

"Rei!" Sensei called.

Lee and Jamie bowed to each other. "Onegai-shimasu, sempai!" Lee shouted.

"Yo-i!"

Lee and Jamie took the ready position. Ready position for sparring was the "passive fighting stance." You stood with your left side to the opponent, your elbows against your ribs, your fists raised. The reason you stood sideways was to make the two most critical targets, your solar plexus and your groin, more difficult to strike.

"Hajime!" Sensei gave the command to begin.

Lee focused his eyes on the base of Jamie's throat, the way he'd learned to do in class. That way you always had a sense of your opponent's entire body. If you looked at their face, you might not see what they were doing with their legs. If you looked down, they could punch you without your seeing it coming. Focusing on the base of the neck gave you the best chance to be aware of everything at once.

Jamie started to circle slowly, keeping her left side to Lee. Her face was absolutely blank, showing no feeling and no fear. Lee lifted his left leg to throw a front snap kick at her ribs. Jamie's right arm shot out so fast that Lee felt it smack against his leg before he saw it. Lee hadn't snapped his leg back quickly enough, the way you were supposed to. Jamie had deflected the blow. Lee would have to try a different technique if he hoped to catch Jamie.

Suddenly, Jamie dropped low and lunged forward with a side squat punch to Lee's ribs. He just barely managed to block when she followed up with a punch to Lee's nose, which was now exposed. Lee threw his arms up to block his face, but he was too late. Jamie landed her technique, stopping her fist just before it touched Lee's face so that she wouldn't injure him.

"Yame!" Sensei stopped them.

Lee and Jamie stepped away from each other, still in passive stance. Anytime one person landed a technique, there was a pause in the sparring.

"Hajime!" Sensei had them start again.

Lee felt humiliated. Not only was Jamie faster than he was, she had complete control. But Lee wasn't going to give up. He stepped towards Jamie and dropped his raised fists towards her collarbone. Jamie defended herself with a double chest block, flinging Lee's arms away like two twigs. With Lee's chest exposed, she quickly drew her elbows back and rammed her fists straight forward into Lee's ribs and solar plexus. Again, she stopped her fists right before she made contact, but she'd scored again because Lee hadn't been able to block.

"Yame!" Sensei stopped them.

Breathing hard, Lee stood up straight, keeping his eyes focused on Jamie's neck. Even though the fight was over, he couldn't bear to look at her face. He didn't feel like he could look anyone in the face after this. Lee had not known what it felt like to lose a sparring match until now. He would have been much happier if he'd never known what it felt like.

"Kio-tsuke! Rei!" Sensei commanded.

Lee stood at attention, then hastily bowed to Jamie. "Arigato, sempai," he mumbled.

"Two more volunteers," Sensei said.

Lee backed into his spot against the wall, barely watching the next two opponents go at it. He couldn't believe what a horrible turn his life had taken in the past twenty-four hours. To think, just yesterday morning, he'd been top deshi, someone all the other kids looked up to. Now he was a loser.

When class was over, Lee dawdled by the water fountain. He couldn't bear to go into the locker room and hear the other guys talking about how badly Jamie had beaten him.

"Great sparring, Jamie," Rosalie Davis said, slapping Jamie on the back of her sweat-soaked gi. "We need more strong girls in the dojo. Girl power!" Rosalie pumped her fist in the air.

Maybe Lee would go into the locker room after all. It couldn't be worse than what he was hearing out here on the deck. Lee trudged across the classroom and stepped through the curtained doorway.

"She made mincemeat out of him . . ." Jeremy was saying as Lee entered the locker room.

Lee didn't hear the rest of the sentence because Michael shot a quick elbow into Jeremy's ribs, silencing him.

"Hi, Lee," Michael said, his face full of sympathy. "How's it going?"

Lee didn't know which was worse, Michael's pity or Jeremy's unflattering description of the fight. "Fine," Lee said glumly, heading for his locker.

"Too bad that new girl beat you," Kevin Whittaker said. He stood facing a mirror, dragging a brush through his curly reddish brown hair. "But I guess it doesn't bother you," he added snidely, "because *kumite's just an exercise.*"

Kevin's words stung almost as badly as losing to Jamie did. A while ago, Lee had sparred with Kevin in class. Of course Lee had beaten him. Kevin was a white belt, much less experienced than Lee. Still, Kevin had been so furious about it that he'd convinced his big brother, Jason, to avenge him by picking a fight with Lee.

Lee hadn't understood at the time why Kevin had been so upset because kumite *was* just an exercise. It wasn't a real fight. But now that Lee had lost, Kevin's reactions made a lot more sense. It felt horrible to be beaten by someone better than you. It made you want to crawl into a hole and disappear.

Chapter Six

After Lee had showered and changed, he bolted from the locker room and rushed across the deck. He wasn't planning to wait for his brothers like he usually did. Not because he was mad at them. It wasn't their fault that they admired Jamie. Lee just needed to get away from people for awhile. It wasn't too cold out, and it was still light. A nice long bicycle ride would be just the thing to clear his mind.

"Lee!" Jamie called to him for the second time that day. Still dressed in her gi, she stood by the makiwara, punching it methodically, her fist landing perfectly on target every time. She wasn't a human being, Lee decided. She was a machine.

"What do you want?" he asked. He was trying to be polite, but somehow it wasn't coming across that way.

"Well, uh . . . nothing really," Jamie said. "I just thought if you weren't doing anything we could talk about Musashi. Not many kids our age know about him."

Lee had had enough of Jamie for one day. The idea of a bike ride was sounding better and better. "Sorry," Lee said, "but I've really got to go. Maybe some other time, OK?"

Jamie nodded, and tightened the knot on her belt. "Sure. See ya."

"See ya." Lee hadn't gone more than a few more feet when he heard his name called again.

"Lee!" Jeremy called, barreling out of the dressing room.

Lee looked longingly at the door. It looked like he'd never get out of here. "What?" he asked his brother, his patience wearing thin.

"I have a karate problem I need to talk to you about," Jeremy said, pushing up his wire-rimmed glasses on his nose.

"Will this take long?" Lee asked. "I'm sort of in a hurry."

"Well, it might take a couple minutes," Jeremy said, "but if you can't talk now we can always talk later."

"Later would be better," Lee said. "Sorry."

"No problem," Jeremy said. "Where are you going?"

"There's something I have to do," Lee said, heading for the doorway at last. "I'll meet you at home."

* * *

What's eating Lee? Jeremy wondered as his brother ran from the dojo. Ever since Jamie had shown up, Lee had been acting really strange. Sure, Jamie was more advanced than Lee, but so were a lot of other people. There were a whole bunch of grown-ups at the dojo who had black belts.

Besides, Lee had no reason to be upset. His life was going perfectly. Sensei had given him permission to test for his black tips. The person who *really* had a problem was Jeremy. Jeremy still hadn't figured out a way to impress Sensei, and time was running out.

Thwak! Thwak!

Jamie Oscarson's knuckles made a sharp cracking sound as she punched the makiwara.

Thwak! Thwak!

The sound was so clear and loud it echoed through the entire dojo. She had such powerful techniques. No wonder Sensei was impressed by her.

The idea came to Jeremy in a brilliant flash. If Sensei was impressed by power, then Jeremy knew exactly what he had to do. And Jamie was just the person to help him.

Thwak! Thwak!

The sound got louder as Jeremy approached Jamie. He stood by politely until she'd finished punching. When she turned to face him, Jeremy bowed to Jamie.

"Onegai-shimasu, sempai," he said.

Jamie bowed back. "Onegai-shimasu," she said.

71

"Do you have a minute?" Jeremy asked. "I'd like to ask you something."

"So what do you think, guys?" Mrs. Jenkins asked a few hours later, after dinner. A petite, physically fit woman in her late thirties, she sat at one end of the kitchen table holding up a large cartoon drawing mounted on a piece of cardboard. The cartoon was a picture of a silver-gray dog with infrared eyes and an antenna for a tail.

"I don't even have to guess who that is," Jeremy said, scooping the last of his chocolate ice cream out of a bowl and licking the spoon. "That's got to be Turbopup, right?"

Mrs. Jenkins tucked a stray strand of coppery red hair behind her ear. Her hair was pulled back into a ponytail, but wisps of hair kept escaping, giving her a wild, distracted look. "Good guess," she said to Jeremy, "but what I need to know is—do you like him? Is he cool? I need to know what all of you think since you're boys and you're the same age as the kids who read Turbotron comics."

Lee stared down at his own bowl of chocolate ice cream, which had now partially melted into chocolate mush. Usually he loved helping his mother with her work. Andrea Jenkins was editor-in-chief of Rocket Comics and the creator of Turbotron, the most popular comic book superhero in the country. Turbotron had the mind of a computer, the heart of a man, and superhuman power which came from his internal, turbo-charged engine.

One of the reasons Turbotron was so popular was that Lee and his brothers acted as kid-consultants to their mother when she brought home her ideas for Turbotron comics. They'd tell her what they liked and didn't like, and she almost always followed their advice. Turbopup was a new character their mom had just created to be a pet for Turbotron.

But tonight, Lee just couldn't work up much enthusiasm for Turbotron, Turbopup, or anything else for that matter. All Lee could think about was how easily Jamie had defeated him in kumite this afternoon. The bike ride hadn't helped. Neither had the chocolate ice cream.

"I like him," Michael said, taking the cartoon of Turbopup from his mom and studying it closely. "The artist did a really good job of making him look three-dimensional. And he looks like a cross between a real dog and a robot."

"That's what we were aiming for," Mrs. Jenkins said, leaning closer to Michael so she could look at the drawing with him. "The tail's not just for looks, either. That's how Turbopup gets long-range transmissions from Turbotron when they're in different galaxies. Turbopup can send messages through his tail, too."

73

Mr. Jenkins, sitting at the opposite end of the table from his wife, got up from his chair and stood behind Michael. Tall and athletic, he had straight blond hair like Michael's, and round, wire-rimmed glasses like Jeremy's. He'd been an army officer and now he was the director of a local recycling center. "He's a cute little fella," Mr. Jenkins said, leaning down so his head was between Michael's and Mrs. Jenkins's. "Only, why don't you call him WonderPup or WonderDog or something like that?"

"Ewwww!" Jeremy said, making a face. "That's a terrible name. And it has nothing to do with Turbotron. Turbopup's much better."

"What do you think?" Mrs. Jenkins asked, holding the cartoon across the table so Lee could take a look at it.

Lee sighed and took the cardboard. He'd barely looked at it before he mumbled, "It's okay, I guess."

Mrs. Jenkins took back the picture and eyed Lee with concern. "Is something the matter, Lee?" she asked.

"Uh-uh." Lee shook his head.

"Call me psychic," Mrs. Jenkins said, pointing to Lee's uneaten bowl of melted ice cream. "But it looks like something's wrong."

Lee forced himself to smile and he spooned up some of the chocolate sauce. "I'm fine," he insisted. "I was just waiting for it to melt. I like it better that way."

Mrs. Jenkins looked like she didn't believe Lee, but she let the subject drop. "So," she said, slipping the Turbopup cartoon back into a manila envelope, "how was karate today?"

"It was great!" Jeremy gushed, picking up his empty bowl and heading across the blue-and-white linoleum floor. He stopped at the counter where the box of chocolate ice cream sat and spooned himself a second helping. "There's this new girl in class who's really helping me a lot. She's a great teacher."

Lee sank a little lower in his chair. Was there no escape from Jamie Oscarson? It was bad enough he had to see her in school and at the dojo, but did he have to be reminded of her at home, too?

"What's she helping you with?" Mr. Jenkins asked, sipping his herbal tea out of a mug that said General Dad.

Jeremy returned to the table and plunked his bowl down. "It's hard to explain to someone who doesn't do karate," he said. "Let's just say it's a special technique. A special, *helpful* technique."

Lee looked up at Jeremy curiously. Jeremy was being awfully mysterious. What were Jeremy and Jamie up to? "I take karate," Lee said to his brother. "Explain this 'helpful' technique to me."

"Sorry," Jeremy said, spooning more chocolate ice cream into his mouth. "Since you couldn't help me, I found someone who could. You'll find out soon, though. That Jamie Oscarson's a great teacher. She really knows her stuff."

"I'll say," Michael agreed. "I'd give anything to be able to paint the way she does."

Lee's throat suddenly felt very tight. He wanted to keep eating the soupy, melted ice cream so his mother wouldn't worry about him, but Lee was afraid he wouldn't be able to swallow.

Lee had never been so depressed in his entire life. He felt like he'd lost everything that ever mattered to him. At least Michael was a good artist, and Jeremy was a science whiz. But being the best at karate was all Lee had. And now, thanks to Jamie, he didn't even have that.

Even worse, watching Jamie made Lee realize what a natural she was. Lee had worked five long years to perfect his techniques. Jamie hadn't worked nearly as hard, yet her techniques were so much better. She must have a special gift Lee just didn't have.

If he earned his black tips, or even a black belt someday, Lee would never be as good as Jamie. So what was the point of testing on Sunday? What was the point of going back to the dojo at all? Maybe he should just quit karate altogether!

Chapter Seven

Lee's stomach growled as he looked at the hot lunches behind the steamy glass in the cafeteria lunch line. It wasn't that any of the choices looked so delicious. It was the usual Wednesday selection. Gray speckled meatloaf drowning in brown gravy. Mounds of gluey white mashed potatoes. Droopy, overboiled green beans.

But Lee hadn't eaten much for dinner last night, and he'd only been able to choke down a few bites of cereal this morning. By now, even the macaroni swimming in goopy, Day-Glo orange cheese was starting to look good.

"I'll have the macaroni," Lee said to the woman behind the counter. After she'd slopped the macaroni on his plate, Lee slid his tray down the chrome railing to beverages, where Jeremy was pulling his usual two containers of chocolate milk out of a bin filled with crushed ice. Michael, just ahead of Jeremy, was paying the cashier for his tuna fish sandwich.

". . . and then she showed me how you're supposed to point your foot in the direction of your next move so you have a better foundation when you snap your hips around," Jeremy was chattering away to Michael. "It really made a lot of moves easier, especially the three-quarter turns in Pinan Shodan and Pinan Nidan."

"So that's how she gets so much power in her hips," Michael said, nodding as the cashier gave him his change. "I was wondering what her trick was."

Jamie again. Wouldn't his brothers ever stop talking about her? Lee's macaroni, which hadn't smelled half bad, was now starting to turn his stomach. "Sensei told us about placing your foot," Lee reminded his brothers. "Jamie's not the one who made it up."

Jeremy slid his tray up to the cashier. "I know," he said, "but it never really hit me before until she explained it. She's a great teacher."

"I know," Lee snapped. "You've only said it about five hundred times."

Jeremy fished around in his pocket and came up with some crumpled dollar bills which he handed to the cashier. "You're in a lousy mood," he remarked. "What's the matter with you?"

"Nothing," Lee said, moving toward the cashier.

"Lee's probably just nervous about testing this

Sunday," Michael said as he waited for Lee to pay for his lunch. "I know I am."

"Just be glad you *are* testing," Jeremy said. "If I knew I was going to test this Sunday, I wouldn't be worried about a thing."

"It's not so important *when* you test," Lee reminded his younger brother. "You'll get your brown tips sooner or later. So don't be upset."

"I'm not upset," Jeremy said with that same mysterious grin he'd had last night at dinner. "Just don't be surprised if sooner is sooner than you think."

"What's that supposed to mean?" Michael asked as the three brothers headed into the cafeteria. Sixth, seventh, and eighth graders screamed and shouted and ran back and forth in the rows between fake wood formica tables. Mr. Rosario, the lunch monitor, chased after them, shouting into a megaphone, telling them to sit down and be quiet.

"So . . ." Jeremy said, purposely changing the subject. "Where should we sit?"

Michael exchanged a look with Lee and shrugged his shoulders. Lee shook his head. Jeremy was definitely up to something, but it didn't look like they'd be able to get any information out of him.

"There's an empty table . . ." Lee started to say, but Jeremy interrupted him with a shout.

"Hey!" Jeremy exclaimed. "There's Jamie!"

Lee stole a look at Jamie, who was sitting by herself,

thumbing through Musashi's *Book of Five Rings*. Jamie must have heard Jeremy because she looked up and waved at them. Pretending he hadn't seen her, Lee started to put his tray down on a nearby table.

"Wait a minute, Lee," Michael said. "Don't you want to sit with Jamie?"

Of course I don't want to sit with her, Lee wanted to say. *She's already made me lose my appetite. If I eat with her, I'll probably throw up!*

"We really should eat with her," Michael said. "She's new and you heard her say she's having a tough time making friends. Plus now she's in our dojo. The least we can do is be nice to her."

"Yeah," Jeremy agreed. "You should get to know her, Lee. You'd really like her."

Lee wasn't going to begin to get into the fact that a few short weeks ago, Jeremy would never even talk to a girl, let alone eat lunch with one. It seemed as if no matter what Lee did to avoid Jamie, she kept worming her way back into his life. And to make things even worse, his brothers were helping her!

Lee couldn't let anyone know how he really felt. It would be worse than being a bad sport. He'd be showing disrespect to his sempai.

"Well?" Michael asked.

Lee shrugged. "I don't care."

"Great!" Jeremy led the way to Jamie's table. "Hi!"

he greeted her, putting his tray down across from her. "Mind if we sit here?"

Jamie's green eyes lit up and she slipped her book into her bookbag. "Hey, y'all," she said happily. "You guys going over to the dojo later?"

"I've got to," Michael said, sitting beside her. "I want to practice as much as I can before I test on Sunday. I'm really afraid I'm going to forget something."

"You won't forget," Jamie said as Lee reluctantly put his tray down next to Jeremy. "After all the time you've put in, the moves are in your body. The best thing is to not even think and just do it on auto-pilot."

"I guess you would know," Jeremy said, opening his first container of chocolate milk and unwrapping his plastic straw. "You're the expert."

Jamie, who was eating corn chips out of a bag, offered some to Lee. "You don't have to take it from me," she said. "Just ask Lee. I'm sure he knows as well as I do."

Lee shook his head, refusing the chips.

"So, Lee," Jamie began, "your knife-hand blocks looked really good yesterday." Knife hands was a technique where your fingers were very straight and stiff and pressed together, with your thumb tucked in tight. You could use knife hands for slicing or chopping attacks. You could also use knife hands to block. "I was admiring you during the Pinan kata," Jamie

81

continued. "You were whipping your hands out so fast I could hear the air whoosh by. I wish I had your speed. What's your secret?"

Jeremy and Michael also turned to Lee to hear his answer.

Lee didn't have an answer. He knew exactly what Jamie was doing. She was trying to be nice because she felt sorry for him after the way she'd beaten him yesterday. But Lee didn't want her pity. Lee stabbed a curl of macaroni with his fork and jammed it into his mouth.

"Lee," Michael prodded him. "Jamie asked you a question."

Lee chewed silently, glaring straight ahead, not looking at Michael or Jamie or Jeremy. The macaroni tasted like sour mud, but at least eating was an excuse not to talk. He didn't trust his voice, anyway. If he did answer Jamie, he might say something really nasty and mean, something he'd regret for a long, long time.

"Lee," Jeremy said, tapping him on the shoulder. "Are you deaf? Jamie's talking to you!"

Relax and breathe, said the voice inside Lee's head, but it was useless. Lee had no control over himself at this moment. He couldn't be calm in the face of the enemy any more than he could win against Jamie at kumite. His five years of karate training had been

82

completely useless. He'd just been kidding himself all along by thinking he was any good.

Lee stood up abruptly and climbed over the bench. "I gotta go," he said.

"Lee!" Michael called after him. "What's wrong?"

Leaving his tray behind and ignoring his brothers, Lee walked right out of the cafeteria. There was only one thing left to do. Today, right after school, he was going to talk to Sensei and hand in his resignation.

My last time, Lee thought as he pushed open the door to the dojo that afternoon. His last time taking off his shoes and placing them in the closet in the entry hall. His last time passing through the front hall covered with photographs of deshi doing their moves. His last time knocking on the door of Sensei Davis to ask if they could talk.

It all still felt so familiar, so much a part of him, that Lee couldn't believe he'd never be coming back. But the way things looked right now, Lee didn't have any other choice.

Sensei Davis was sitting behind his beat-up old desk, wearing his gi and reading a book called *The Essence of Okinawan Karate-Do.* Lee had read that book, too. It was written by Shoshin Nagamine, the master who'd founded their style of karate. Nagamine, who was still alive and practicing karate in

KARATE CLUB

Okinawa, was a tenth-degree blackbelt, the highest level. His book gave a history of their style and had photographs of him demonstrating all the basic techniques and kata in their system.

"Hi, Lee," Sensei said, without even looking up from his book. Sensei always did that, but it never failed to startle Lee. Sensei was so aware of what was around him that he could see things without looking directly at them. Lee hoped he could become that aware someday . . .

No, Lee corrected himself. This was his last day at karate. Soon he wouldn't even remember Sensei, let alone try to be like him.

"Would you like to talk?" Sensei asked, looking up from his book. "We still have a while before class."

Lee nodded and bowed. "Arigato, Sensei," he said quietly, moving towards the straight-backed wooden chair and sitting down.

Sensei shut his book and his bright, dark eyes looked straight into Lee's. "It's interesting how quickly things can change," he said.

Lee's eyes opened wide. He hadn't even said anything, yet Sensei seemed already to know why he was here. Or was Sensei's comment coincidental? Maybe Sensei was just passing along a bit of wisdom.

"Do you know why we don't compete in tournaments in our style of karate?" Sensei asked, leaning forward on his desk.

Lee relaxed. Sensei wasn't a mind reader. Sensei was just making conversation. "No, Sensei," Lee said.

"Because karate's not a competitive sport," Sensei said. "At least not the way Master Nagamine envisioned it. Tournaments focus on winning points and trophies. Tournaments focus on defeating another person, not turning inward and defeating the enemy inside yourself. It's more important to think about perfecting your own techniques than about what other people are doing."

Lee didn't completely understand what Sensei was saying, but he was beginning to suspect that Sensei wasn't making random conversation after all. Maybe it was the word *competitive* or the fact that Sensei had brought up the idea of defeating another person. Was Sensei actually talking about Lee and Jamie?

"So, what have you come to tell me, Lee?" Sensei asked.

There was no doubt about it anymore. Sensei knew. Sensei knew Lee had been psyched out by Jamie. Sensei probably even knew Lee had come here today to tell him he was quitting.

"It's not that I don't like karate," Lee began, avoiding Sensei's steady gaze. "I mean, karate's my *life!*"

"But . . ." Sensei prompted.

Lee looked down at the floor. "Well, karate's the sort of thing where you have to give it your all. If you're only going to do it halfway, then you shouldn't even bother."

"And?" Sensei asked.

"Well," Lee said, looking up and catching Sensei's eye again, "lately I've been wondering whether I have what it takes to be the best."

Sensei leaned back in his chair and stroked his sandy mustache. "I'm a little confused," he said. "You're not sure you can *be* the best, or you're not sure you can *do* your best?"

Lee thought hard before he answered Sensei's question. There was a difference between being the best person in the class and giving karate your best effort. But at this point, Lee wasn't sure he could do either.

Sensei stood up and moved around to the front of his desk, where Lee was sitting. "I want to show you something," Sensei said, heading for the door leading back to the front hallway.

Lee followed Sensei into the hall, to the door that led to the classroom. Inside the classroom, several kids in uniform were already warming up. Just outside the door was a small bronze plaque. Sensei pointed to the plaque, and Lee read it:

Leave your ego at the door.

"Do you know what that means?" Sensei asked Lee.

"I think so," Lee said. "People with big egos are

conceited, so the quote probably means you're not supposed to show off or brag or try to be better than anybody else when you're on the deck."

"That's one meaning," Sensei agreed, crossing his burly arms across his chest. "But it also means you shouldn't worry about whether someone else is better than you or let it get you down."

Lee heaved a deep, anxious breath.

Sensei reached into the shoe closet and pulled out a clean rag. He polished the bronze plaque with the rag. "There are other meanings, too," Sensei said as he wiped. "It means you shouldn't act with jealousy and resentment just because you think someone is better than you. It means you shouldn't let yourself get so wrapped up in your own problems that you stop thinking about how other people might feel."

Like the way I've been ignoring Jeremy, Lee thought, remembering how badly his brother had wanted to test. Lee had been so worried about Jamie that he hadn't thought much about what Jeremy was probably going through right now. He'd asked Lee for help, and Lee had told him he was too busy. It hadn't even been true!

But that wasn't the worst thing he'd done these past few days. Lee had been unfriendly, even rude to Jamie every time he'd seen her when she'd been perfectly nice to him.

But what about my *problems?* Lee demanded of

himself. *Don't I have a right to be upset, too?* He'd been going along, minding his own business, then Jamie had come and ruined his life. And Lee *wasn't* competing with her. He was willing to step aside so she could take his place as the best kid at the dojo. There was nothing unreasonable about that.

"Arigato, Sensei," Lee said. "But I'm not competing with anyone else. It's just that now there is a more advanced brown belt, a brown belt with black tips. She is much better than me. So much better that I know I can never be as good. I don't think there's any point for me to continue."

"There's a difference between hearing and listening," Sensei said evenly.

Lee was confused. "Yes, Sensei?" he said respectfully.

"If you really believe that you can't continue to improve yourself, you have forgotten what you've learned. In karate, it doesn't matter who's best. It matters to be *your* best. It matters to always be open to learning more, to be willing to work hard, to always try to do better—not just in karate, in your life."

Lee was beginning to feel like he'd been very selfish—and maybe not very honest with himself, either. He thought he understood what Sensei was trying to say. Karate had been the most important part of his life for five years. Could he really give it up so easily, just because Jamie had better techniques than he did?

Maybe he was being too hasty deciding to quit. Maybe he could give it another chance. Maybe he could ignore Jamie and just focus on himself.

"Arigato, Sensei," Lee said, bowing. "I guess I'll get ready for class now, if that's OK with you."

Sensei also bowed. "Arigato," he said.

Lee stepped through the doorway and bowed to the shinden wall. Part of him was happy that he hadn't given up karate, but another part of him felt heavy, like lead. He'd keep coming to class and doing his best, but he didn't feel the way he used to. His heart wasn't in it.

"Lee!"

Lee turned and saw Jeremy, already in his gi, punching the makiwara in the back of the room.

Lee waved at Jeremy as he walked across the deck.

"Wait a minute!" Jeremy called, gesturing Lee to come over. "I want to show you something."

Lee sighed. He was curious to hear about Jeremy's idea, but he was also a little annoyed at Jeremy for going on about Jamie all the time. Lee thought about what Sensei had said about trying to think about other people, not just yourself. "I'll be out in a minute," Lee promised. "Just let me change into my gi."

"Your loss," Jeremy said quietly as he watched Lee duck behind the curtain leading to the men's locker room. Jeremy wasn't angry at Lee. He'd just thought

Lee might enjoy what was about to happen, but it didn't really matter if he missed it. The one thing Jeremy knew for sure was that he just couldn't wait any longer to carry out his brilliant plan.

Even without Lee, Jeremy was going to have a pretty good-sized audience. Michael and Dwight Vernon were practicing *Pinan Sandan,* the third green-belt kata, and Jamie Oscarson was working with some of the new white belts. Jon Walker was doing knuckle push-ups on the matted deck, and Rosalie Davis was doing bicep curls with ten-pound dumb-bells. The only person missing was Sensei, but he should be out any minute, and that was when the show would begin.

It would be a very short show, but Jeremy knew it would prove to Sensei, once and for all, that Jeremy was ready to test for his brown tips. Jeremy now realized that it wasn't enough to know all the kata and prearranged fighting sequences for his level. He had to show super-special spirit. He had to prove he could do the hardest thing of all, something you only got to do at promotions, something that showed you weren't afraid of anything.

Jeremy checked the clock on the wall. Class would be starting soon, which meant Sensei might come out of his office at any minute. Jeremy had to set up quickly.

Scooting over to the side of the room, Jeremy hefted one of the large, gray cinderblocks stacked along the wall. The thing must have weighed fifteen pounds, at least. Carrying it towards the center of the wooden deck, Jeremy set it down. Then he went back to the wall and picked up another cinderblock the same size as the first. Sweating from the effort, Jeremy lugged the second cinderblock across the floor and set it down about a foot from the first. Phase one was done. Now it was time for phase two.

Heading back to the spot where he'd gotten the cinderblocks, Jeremy picked up four identical pieces of wood, each about three quarters of an inch thick. Jeremy jogged with these back to the cinderblocks. He stacked them on top of each other and, very carefully, put the planks across the two cinderblocks.

As Jeremy stared down at the pile of wood, he tried not to be scared. After all, he'd broken two boards at his last promotion, when he tested for green belt. This couldn't be that much harder. And think how impressed Sensei would be. Boys testing for brown tips only had to break three boards. If Jeremy could break four, Sensei wouldn't have any more reason to hold him back from testing.

Jeremy glanced towards the curtained doorway leading from the classroom to Sensei's office. So where was Sensei, already? Jeremy felt so ready to do this he was afraid he might go through with it before Sensei showed up. But that would be dumb. If Sensei wasn't there to watch, there'd be no point in doing it in the first place.

The black curtain fluttered. Jeremy saw Sensei's hand pull it aside as he entered the deck in his uniform.

Jamie Oscarson instantly snapped to attention. "Shotu-mate!" she called. Everyone immediately stopped whatever they were doing. Jeremy stood up straight and tall.

"Sensei ni mawate!" Jamie shouted, and everyone turned to Sensei. "Sensei ni rei!" Jamie shouted.

Everyone bowed to Sensei. "Onegai-shimasu, Sensei!" they yelled.

Jeremy only had seconds to act. The next thing Sensei was going to do was give the command for everyone to line up. It was now or never.

Jeremy took his pose, just like Jamie had shown him. He placed his left foot in front of the left cinderblock and angled his right foot back in line with the center of the boards. Then he stiffened his right hand into a tight knife hand, fingers pressed together, and raised his hand above his head.

Don't think about hitting the boards, Jamie's voice reminded him. *Aim for a point* below *the boards. Pretend they're a stack of crackers and think about slicing* through *them*.

Jeremy breathed deeply through his nose. He summoned up all his power and energy and tried to focus it into his right hand. Then, with a sharp exhale, Jeremy gave an earsplitting kiai—*"Hyaaaaaaah!"*— and struck the boards as hard as he could.

Chapter Eight

Lee had been hurrying as fast as he could. He was still tying his brown belt when he heard Jamie call the class to attention. He better get out there. There was only about a minute left to line up.

Then he heard a terrific kiai. He looked up, startled. What was going on out there? Had he missed something?

He heard the second cry just as he was pushing the curtain to step onto the deck.

"Uhn!"

It was Jeremy! Lee could see him at the back of the room. Jeremy lay on the floor, clutching his arm, his face creased with pain. Sensei was already halfway across the deck, rushing towards Jeremy, and Michael was right behind him. Lee, too, ran as fast as he could towards his younger brother.

"What happened?" Sensei Davis asked as he knelt beside Jeremy.

Lee, arriving at the back of the room at the same time as Sensei, already knew the answer. The two cement blocks and the pile of wooden boards, still balanced between them, said it all. Jeremy had tried—and failed—to break the boards. The question was, why? The only time deshi were supposed to break boards was at a promotion.

"Oohhh," Jeremy moaned. Two slow, fat tears rolled down his face. "It really hurts."

Lee knelt down on the other side of Jeremy and took a look at Jeremy's right hand, which Sensei was cradling in his larger one. The right side of Jeremy's hand, between the pinkie knuckle and the wrist, was purplish-red and starting to swell.

Sensei looked at Lee, his face grave. "Get the first-aid kit," he instructed Lee. "I think your brother's broken a bone."

Lee hopped to his feet and took off across the deck, whizzing passed Jamie and Dwight and Rosalie and all the other kids still heading towards Jeremy. He still didn't understand what had happened, but he knew that this must have been the mysterious thing Jeremy had been talking about since yesterday. Jeremy had mentioned Jamie had something to do with this, too, but Lee still couldn't figure out what.

Dashing through the curtain that led to Sensei's office, Lee searched the room for the first-aid kit. He found it on a shelf next to Sensei's desk, behind

Sensei's *dai-sho*, his two samurai swords. Lee carefully moved the swords, valuable antiques Sensei had received as a gift from the adult black belts, and pulled the green metal case off the shelf. The case was heavy, but Lee barely felt the weight as he pushed through the curtain again and sped towards the back of the dojo.

"Cold pack, please," Sensei Davis said as Lee skidded to a halt. Lee dropped down to the floor and opened the first aid kit. He found a white plastic rectangular package filled with something squishy. "Twist it like you're wringing a wet washcloth," Sensei told Lee. "That's how you make it cold."

Lee didn't see how this could work, but he followed Sensei's orders. Sure enough, he started to feel a chill creep through the plastic. Lee handed the cold pack to Sensei, who wrapped it around Jeremy's right hand.

"Hold it there," Sensei told Jeremy. "It's important to keep the break cold, to minimize swelling."

"It might not be broken," Jeremy said, rubbing his wet cheeks against the shoulders of his uniform. "It doesn't hurt as much as I thought."

Sensei stood up, towering over Jeremy and Lee. "Believe me," he said. "It's broken. I can tell by the swelling. I've broken that same bone myself, twice."

Jeremy's blue eyes started to fill again. "But I don't want to have a broken hand. I want to do karate."

Sensei shrugged. "Come to my office. We have to call your parents."

Lee helped Jeremy to his feet. "I'll come with you," he said.

Michael fell into step on Jeremy's other side. "Me too."

Jamie, who'd been standing off to the side, watching quietly, moved towards the pile of boards and carried them back to the side of the room where Sensei usually kept them.

"Mom and Dad are going to kill me," Jeremy groaned as they followed Sensei past the curious eyes of the other deshi.

"What did you think you were doing back there? Showing off?" Michael whispered.

"I don't want to talk about it right now," Jeremy said, nodding his head towards Sensei's back. "I'll tell you later."

When they got inside Sensei's office, Sensei was already looking through his card file for Jeremy's address. "Who do you want me to call?" he asked. "Your father or your mother?"

"Call our dad," Lee volunteered. "He works right here in town. Our mom works in the city, so it would take her longer to get here."

Sensei nodded and picked up the phone. While he was breaking the bad news to their father, Jeremy removed the cold pack so he could look at his hand. "Whoa," he exclaimed, showing off his hand. "It looks so weird!"

Lee had to agree. Even with the cold pack, the right side of Jeremy's hand had swollen up so much it looked like there was a Ping-Pong ball beneath the skin. Lee thought back to what Sensei had said earlier about fighting the enemy within yourself. It looked like Jeremy had fought that battle and lost—big time.

"Your dad will be here in a few minutes," Sensei said, hanging up the phone. "You boys can wait here in my office until he comes. Meanwhile, I'm going to start class. When your dad gets here, let me know. I know a good doctor who specializes in sports injuries and broken bones."

"Arigato, Sensei," Lee said as Sensei headed back into the classroom.

As soon as Sensei was out of the room, Lee turned to Jeremy. "OK," he said. "Out with it. What were you doing with those boards? What were you trying to prove?"

Jeremy hung his head. "You don't have to yell. I'm feeling bad enough as it is."

"And whose fault is that?" Michael wanted to know. "Nobody made you do it."

"I know, I know," Jeremy said, staring at the cold pack. "But you have to understand. I was just trying to show Sensei I was ready to test for my brown tips.

I figured once he saw me break, he'd change his mind."

"You broke all right," Lee said, dropping down onto Sensei's mangy red couch that looked like a reject from the Salvation Army. "But even if you'd split those boards in two, it wouldn't have changed Sensei's mind. Don't you know that? Breaking boards has nothing to do with being ready for promotion."

Jeremy shook his head, crestfallen.

Of course Jeremy wouldn't know that, a voice in Lee's head chided him. *He's only a green belt. He still doesn't know all the ins and outs of promotions. But* you *could have told him if you'd bothered to listen to him when he asked for your help. You could have stopped him before he hurt himself. This whole thing* is *your fault.*

Come to think of it, Jeremy's behavior hadn't been all too different from Lee's these past few days. They'd both done something stupid because of bruised egos. Jeremy's break had come from the same place as Lee's desire to quit karate.

"I thought I knew what I was doing," Jeremy said glumly, unwrapping the cold pack so he could take another look at his swollen hand. "Jamie worked with me for half an hour yesterday on breaking technique. I thought I had it down."

Jamie! So that was the connection! Maybe this whole thing wasn't Lee's fault after all. Maybe Jamie wasn't the perfect deshi Lee had made her out to be. Jamie should have known better than to encourage Jeremy to break boards. Why, Jamie had practically broken Jeremy's hand herself!

Lee stood up. "I knew Jamie was up to no good," he said, gritting his teeth. "I'm going to go out there and tell her a thing or two."

"You can't!" Jeremy shouted, jumping up. "Class already started."

Lee peeked through the curtain and saw that Sensei was leading the class through warm-ups. Jeremy was right. Lee couldn't barge in now.

A few minutes later, Mr. Jenkins peered in through the doorway that led from the front hall. He wore a T-shirt and jeans, as he always did at work, and his brown eyes were worried behind his wire-rimmed glasses. "Jeremy!" he exclaimed when he saw his sons. "Are you OK?"

Jeremy ran to his dad. "I'll be fine," he said. "I just need to see a doctor. Sensei Davis will give you the name."

"Okay," Mr. Jenkins said. He looked at Lee and Michael. "You guys want to come?" he asked.

Much as Lee wanted to wait for Jamie, he couldn't abandon his brother now. He'd have to talk to Jamie tomorrow, at school.

"Sure," Lee said to his father. "I just need two minutes to change."

* * *

She's avoiding me, Lee told himself Thursday afternoon as he roamed the halls of Midvale Middle School. Before school, at lunchtime, and now, after school, he'd stuck his head inside the door of every classroom. He'd gone up and down every stairwell. He'd circled the outside of the school three times trying to find Jamie Oscarson and have it out with her for what she'd done to Jeremy. But the perfect deshi was defending herself perfectly by not being there when the attack came.

"Where *is* she?" Lee muttered as he headed for the back door of the sixth-grade wing. It was almost three o'clock. He couldn't afford to spend any more time searching the school. If he wanted to yell at her, he'd have to wait until he got to karate class.

A blast of cold wind slapped Lee in the face as he pushed open the double doors of the sixth-grade wing. The sky was gray. The leafless trees surrounding the football field looked like skeleton fingers.

At first Lee didn't notice Jamie by the bike rack because she was crouched between two of the tangled bicycles, trying to pry hers loose from the one next to it. She wore scuffed cowboy boots, jeans, and a dirty gray hooded sweatshirt. Over the sweatshirt, she wore a brown leather jacket with a rip in one sleeve. With her straggly hair poking out from under her raised hood, she looked more like a boy than a girl.

And if Lee hadn't been so furious with her, he might have thought it was funny that her handlebars had somehow gotten stuck in the front wheel of the next bicycle.

But it wasn't funny. Jamie was too dangerous to laugh at. She'd completely ruined Lee's life, and now she was trying to ruin Jeremy's, too. Jeremy wasn't coming to karate today, or any other day for the next eight weeks, because his right hand was in a cast. The doctor had said Jeremy had broken the fifth right metacarpal in his right hand, the bone between the pinkie knuckle and the wrist. The cast was going to be on for three weeks, and then Jeremy had to wait five more weeks before he could do any physical activity with his hand.

Lee still blamed himself for not being there when Jeremy needed him, but it was Jamie's fault even more. And now it was time for Jamie to pay the price.

With a ferocious tug, Jamie pulled her bicycle free, scraping off more of the yellow paint on its frame. Then she turned and noticed Lee.

"Hey!" she called to him in a friendly tone. "How's Jeremy's hand? I was really worried about him yesterday."

"Oh, sure you were," Lee retorted, marching up to her. "You were probably laughing all the way home from the dojo."

"I don't know what you're talking about," Jamie said quietly.

"Don't be such a hypocrite. You know perfectly well what I'm talking about. You're on a campaign to finish off the Jenkins family. First me, then Jeremy . . . I guess Michael's next, right? I guess it's a good thing he's got art class today, or he'd have to watch out." Lee took a few steps closer to Jamie, pausing just inches from her.

Jamie didn't step back or seem alarmed at Lee's threatening tone. In fact, her face became very peaceful and Lee noticed her taking smooth, deep breaths. "I have nothing against your family," she said, gazing at him with her wide-set green eyes. "I think all of you are really nice guys."

Lee snorted. "You have a pretty weird way of showing it. Where do you come off taking advantage of a lower-ranking student and setting him up to hurt himself that way?"

"I didn't set him up—"

"Don't give me that. If it weren't for you, Jeremy never would have pulled that stupid stunt. My only question is, what did you say to trick him into it? Did you tell him you were sharing some deep karate secret? Did you dare him to do it?" Lee was warming up to this now. He barely felt the gusty wind that whipped at his down parka.

Jamie was still breathing calmly, but her eyes showed a glimmer of unhappiness. "I didn't tell him to do anything," she said. "He asked me to show him the correct technique for breaking, so I did. I thought he was preparing for promotion, not planning to do what he did."

"You'll say anything to protect yourself, won't you?" Lee snapped. "Not that I blame you. You may have fooled Sensei into thinking you're the perfect karate student, but you haven't fooled me. I know what you really are."

Jamie crossed her arms across her chest, and the corners of her lips turned downwards. "Oh?" she asked, her voice shaking a little.

Lee felt like his whole body was filled with poison, and now it rose to the surface. "You're a show-off and a liar. You're a slob with messy hair and dirty clothes." The words sounded mean even to Lee, but he couldn't stop himself anymore. All the anger and frustration that had built up over the past four days came pouring out now in a flood he couldn't stop. "You think you're so great just because you have a brown belt with black tips. You think you can come out of nowhere and just take over the dojo. You'll do anything to make sure you stay on top, even if it means hurting other people . . ."

Lee would have said more, but a loud "Yahooo!"

interrupted him. Then there was another "Yahooo!" closer and louder. Lee looked over Jamie's shoulder and his heart lurched. Coasting down the hill were those four guys on the two bicycles, the troublemakers from the other day. Mr. Cefari might have scared them off, but not for long.

Quickly, Lee moved past Jamie to the bike rack and unlocked his bicycle. He wheeled it backwards, wanting to get out of there before they got any closer. Not that he was running away. It would just be easier to avoid them altogether. Jamie seemed to have the same idea. She straddled her bicycle and started pedaling towards the break in the fence that led to the road.

The bike with Bloody Dagger and Motorcycle Boots on it skidded around in front of her, blocking her exit. The other bike, with Skull and a guy with his head shaved except for a little hair on top, screeched to a halt in front of Lee.

"Not so fast," Skull said, hopping off the bike and grabbing Lee's handlebars. "Where do you think you're going?"

Lee's heart started pumping faster as he stared into Skull's narrowed, glittering eyes. "None of your business," he said in a controlled voice.

Skull laughed. "Listen to the little boy talk big."

Lee hated when people made fun of his size. Even

though he was twelve, he was still a half inch shorter than Jeremy who was only eleven. Lee felt his fists clench.

"Enough words," Skull said. "It's time for action." Skull jerked Lee's bicycle out of Lee's grasp. Lee leaped forward, trying to regain his hold on the bicycle, but Shaved Head cut behind him, pinning Lee's arms down against his sides.

Skull jumped on Lee's bicycle, and Lee was helpless to stop him. He couldn't break out of Shaved Head's viselike grip. Meanwhile, Bloody Dagger was pulling Jamie off her bike while Motorcycle Boots took it.

"Do we really want this one?" Motorcycle Boots asked, making a face at the dents and peeling yellow paint on Jamie's bike. "It's a piece of junk!"

"Let go of my bike," Jamie said in a loud, clear voice while Bloody Dagger held her arms behind her back. "It doesn't belong to you."

Skull, riding in a circle on Lee's red ten-speed, laughed. "It does now."

Lee looked desperately around for Mr. Cefari. If there was ever a time he wanted to see the vice principal, it was now.

Jamie struggled in the arms of Bloody Dagger, trying to get away from him.

"We got a fighter here," Bloody Dagger said in a sarcastic voice. "Whoa. Watch out."

Skull smiled. "Give up," he told Jamie. "You haven't got a chance against one of us, forget about four!"

"If I'm forced to defend myself," she said calmly, "I'll neutralize you."

"Ha!" Skull said, dropping Lee's bike with a crash. "You're crazy!"

"I'd advise you not to make a move against me," Jamie said. "It's really not in your best interest."

"Is that a challenge?" Skull asked with an evil smile.

"Just a fact," Jamie replied.

The smile vanished from Skull's face. "OK," he said. "You want to prove how tough you are? Here's your chance." He moved menacingly towards Jamie.

Chapter Nine

"Leave her alone!" Lee shouted. Moments before he'd considered Jamie his worst enemy. It wasn't that he felt any differently now, but it wasn't fair for four big guys to gang up on her. No matter what Jamie had done to him or Jeremy, she didn't deserve this.

"Shut up," Shaved Head said, tightening his grip on Lee's arms. "Who is she? Your girlfriend?"

Lee watched in horror as Skull raised his right leg to kick Jamie. Jamie, meanwhile, was held motionless by Bloody Dagger.

"Don't!" Lee shouted.

Lee couldn't have guessed what was coming. Neither, apparently, did Skull. Like a flash, Jamie's right leg swept forward, striking Skull's leg and knocking it out of the way before he could land the kick. In the same second, using the same foot, she kicked again, hard, to the inside of his supporting left leg, just above the knee.

"Unhh!" Skull grunted and he fell forward, clutching his leg.

Jamie didn't lose any time. Stepping forward on her left foot to get a little more distance from Bloody Dagger and crouching down to loosen his grip, she jammed her right elbow into Dagger's solar plexus and punched him in the nose with her left fist. Lee had seen that move a million times before. It was from Pinan Sandan, the third green-belt kata. But Lee had never seen anybody use it in an actual fight.

"Aaah!" Bloody Dagger shouted, grabbing his face as a trickle of blood dripped out of his nose.

Motorcycle Boots dropped Jamie's bike and lunged at her, trying to grab her arms, which were now free. Jamie did the double chest block from Fukyugata Ni, the second white-belt kata, then landed a double punch to his ribs and stomach. As he bent over in pain, Jamie followed up with an elbow strike to his face. Motorcycle Boots staggered backwards and fell flat on his back.

Lee didn't get to see what happened next to Jamie, because Shaved Head went on the offensive. "Where'd you midgets learn that stuff?" he sneered. "Watching Bruce Lee?" His arms, which had been wrapped around Lee's chest, holding down Lee's arms, now moved up towards Lee's neck.

Lee had to defend himself, and Shaved Head's looser grip gave him the opening he needed. With a piercing kiai, he dropped low, stepped forward, and did a powerful right back kick to Shaved Head's right knee.

Craaaack!

Shaved Head moaned in pain as he dropped to the pavement.

Meanwhile, Bloody Nose, as Lee now thought to call him, had recovered slightly. After wiping his nose on the sleeve of his denim jacket, he hopped on Lee's bike and pedaled straight towards Lee, trying to run him down. Lee instantly saw what he had to do. He stepped sideways and, as Bloody Nose sped past, Lee aimed a high kick at his ribs, knocking him off balance.

Jamie, somehow, had managed to get on the other side of Bloody Nose. As he and Lee's bike fell towards her, she was waiting. She grabbed Bloody Nose off the bike as he fell, jamming her knee into his face. He collapsed onto the sidewalk.

Lee didn't have time to cheer, though, because Skull was up again. He limped towards Lee and started to throw a roundhouse punch so slow and circular that Lee had time to land three punches to the guy's face. Skull's punch never landed. He yowled in pain and dropped to his knees.

It was suddenly very quiet, Lee noticed. Peaceful, almost, except for the moans of the four boys lying along the concrete path. They looked like wounded soldiers on a battlefield. Bloody Nose was clutching his stomach, Shaved Head was grabbing at his knee, and the other two just lay there gasping. Lee's and Jamie's bicycles were on the ground nearby, wheels spinning.

It was a complete and total victory! They'd been outnumbered, and their opponents had been a lot bigger than they were, but none of that had mattered. Lee and Jamie had had their kata, and that's what counted. Everything the old karate masters had said was true. By practicing the kata over and over again, the moves had become instinctive.

Lee wanted to jump up and down and cheer and shake his fists. Those creeps wouldn't mess with them again! But now that the fight was over, Lee was starting to remember how he'd felt right before it started. He'd just about told Jamie to drop dead. Now he really owed her because she'd been the one to do most of the damage. If Lee had been by himself, he might not have even had the presence of mind to fight so many attackers. It was watching Jamie fight so fearlessly that had inspired him.

Lee hated being indebted to Jamie, but he also couldn't help feeling good about what had happened. They hadn't struck first. They'd merely defended themselves. And they'd won.

"Way to go, Jamie!" Lee said, raising his hand to give her a high-five.

Jamie didn't see Lee's hand because she was staring down at four boys lying on the ground. She'd put up her gray hood again, against the cold wind, and her fists were shoved into the pockets of her brown leather jacket. Her face didn't show the happiness Lee was feeling. In fact, she looked very upset.

"What's the matter?" Lee asked.

Jamie turned to look at Lee, and she shivered. Then, without saying a word to Lee, she walked towards Skull, who still lay flat on his back.

"I'm very sorry that I hurt you," Jamie said. "I tried to warn you, and I was just trying to defend myself."

Skull turned his head slightly to look at her. His lip curled. "Bull," he said bitterly.

"Can I help you?" Jamie asked, turning to Bloody Nose. She pulled a clean tissue out of her pocket. "Here," she said, offering it to him. "Your nose is still bleeding."

"Get out of my face," Bloody Nose said, struggling to sit up. He yanked the tissue out of her hand.

"Yeah," said Motorcycle Boots. "Get lost!"

Looking more troubled than she had at any point during the fight, Jamie walked over to her bicycle and picked it up off the ground. She checked it first, to see if it was in working order.

"I really am very sorry," she repeated.

When no one answered her, she slung her right leg over the seat of her bicycle and rode away.

Lee didn't get it. How could Jamie act so nice to people who'd just tried to rob her and beat her up? She should have been furious. Or at least happy that she and Lee had defeated these guys.

Skull and the others were starting to move now. Lee doubted they'd try anything else, but he didn't want to stick around and find out. Besides, karate class started in twenty minutes. If he wanted to get there in time, he'd have to leave now.

"Jamie!" Lee called to her as he picked up his bike and stepped on the pedals. "Wait up!"

Jamie had already turned right and was coasting down the hill past the sprawling red brick school. Lee pedaled frantically to catch up, pulling alongside her.

"Wasn't that great?" he asked, breathing hard. "I loved the part where you caught that guy as he fell off my bike and kneed him. He'll think twice about picking on younger kids next time. Or maybe, after this, there won't be a next time. What a victory!"

Jamie shook her head. "It wasn't a victory," she said, glancing quickly at Lee. "I'm so ashamed."

"Ashamed?" Lee asked. "Are you crazy? We didn't do anything wrong. They struck first. They deserved what they got."

Jamie and Lee coasted around the bend to the right, past the front entrance to their school and the teacher's parking lot.

"The greatest victory," Jamie said, "would have been to avoid the fight altogether. But I'm not blaming you. I'm only blaming myself because I couldn't figure out another way to stop those guys."

"I know that's what karate philosophy's all about," Lee said as they turned left onto a street of split-level houses. "But things don't always work out that way. There are people who don't understand anything but force. I learned that the hard way with Jason Whittaker, and Michael learned it with this guy Todd we met at a comic book convention. We tried to find ways to avoid fighting these guys, but we ran out of options. Karate philosophy doesn't always work in real-life situations."

"I don't believe that," Jamie said. They stopped at a stop sign and stepped, momentarily, off the pedals while a bunch of cars crossed the intersection. "Karate *is* real life. It's my life, anyway. Since I couldn't avoid the fight, it proves how much further I have to go in karate. It means I have that much more to learn."

"Are you kidding?" Lee exclaimed as the last car passed. They stepped back onto their pedals and crossed the intersection. "You're already there in karate. You're so good you don't even have to work at it. Karate just comes naturally to you."

Jamie snorted. "Naturally? *Naturally?!*" She started to laugh hysterically.

Lee got mad. Here he was, trying to make up for all the nasty things he'd said before, and she was making fun of him. Maybe all the things he'd said had been true. Maybe he'd been stupid to think they could ever be anything but enemies.

"Forget I said anything," Lee grumbled. He tried to pedal faster to get away from her.

"There's nothing natural about it," Jamie insisted, keeping up with him. "You don't know anything about me, do you?"

"I know what I see in class," Lee muttered.

"And do you know how many classes I go to every week?" Jamie asked.

Lee shrugged. "I don't know. Three? Four?"

"Six," Jamie said. "Six regular classes. And I practice at home two hours *every day*."

Lee was stunned. He took his eyes off the road momentarily to look at Jamie. The wind had whipped the hood off her head, and her dark hair whipped around her face.

"No way," he said. "Nobody practices that much."

"I do," Jamie said. "And you know why? 'Cause when I first started karate, I was a total klutz. I could hardly tell my left foot from my right. But I really loved it, so I kept working at it."

Lee shook his head in disbelief. "You make it look so easy!"

Jamie grinned. "Have you ever heard of Sensei Baker, from the Philadelphia dojo?"

Lee nodded. "Sensei Davis talks about her sometimes. She's coming Sunday to the promotion, right?"

"I think so," Jamie said. "Well, anyway, Sensei Baker made up a very good quote that we had on our bulletin board in North Carolina. Sensei Baker said: 'Through hard work, things come easily.' But I don't just work on my techniques. I read every book I can find on karate history and philosophy because it helps me control my temper."

Now Lee was really floored. *"You* have a temper? But you seem to have so much self-control."

"Don't be fooled by appearances," Jamie said. She took off down the back road that led to the Midvale Mall. As Lee watched her pull ahead, he realized something important. Jamie was starting to seem like a real person, not a perfect being. It wasn't the stain on the back of her jacket or the fact that the rear fender of her bicycle was bent up at a funny angle. It was knowing that Jamie was as good as she was because she'd worked hard, not because she'd been given some magical gift Lee didn't have.

And this gave Lee hope. He still wasn't anywhere near as good as she was, but he might get there someday. Maybe he'd end up being even better. He just had to keep training and stay focused.

But the most important thing right now was to get

ready for the big promotion. It was only three days away. Lee was prepared to practice every minute of every day, if necessary. It wasn't just because he wanted to earn his black tips. Even more, it was to prove to Sensei that he wasn't a quitter. If anything, he realized, he was more dedicated to karate than ever.

Chapter Ten

"Unhhhh," Michael moaned as he slumped in the backseat of Mr. Jenkins's Jeep at ten o'clock on Sunday morning. He sat in the middle, between Lee and Jeremy, as the Jeep bounced over a rut in the road. Mr. Jenkins was driving, and Mrs. Jenkins sat in the front seat, hastily applying some makeup. The promotion wasn't due to start for another hour, but Lee had rushed everyone out the door. He wanted plenty of time to warm up and run through all his kata before the actual testing started.

Michael moaned again. "I feel sick."

"It's probably because you didn't eat any breakfast," Mrs. Jenkins said, turning around, her open lipstick in one hand, a small mirror in the other. "I wish you'd at least eaten some toast. How are you going to be able to concentrate if you're hungry?"

"I tried, Mom!" Michael insisted, "but I couldn't get it down. It tasted funny."

"You're just nervous," Lee counseled his brother. "This happened at your last two promotions, remember? And you did fine both times." Lee almost laughed at how calm and in control he sounded. He hadn't eaten more than a few bites himself this morning because he was just as nervous as Michael.

"Unhhh . . . " Michael sank down further in his seat and leaned his head back against the leather cushion.

"You'll be fine," Jeremy said to Michael, though he didn't look at his brother. He just stared glumly out the window as they pulled into the Midvale Mall parking lot.

Jeremy's right arm was wrapped from hand to elbow in an Ace bandage which covered a plaster half-cast. His right pinkie was separated from the other fingers, resting on a curved support. The doctor had let Lee and Michael watch while he set Jeremy's break. The doctor said that since Jeremy had broken his metacarpal bone, the joints above and below it—the finger and the wrist—had to be immobilized.

Jeremy had been having trouble doing even the most basic stuff without the use of his right hand. He was adapting pretty fast, though. He was learning how to eat and write and brush his teeth with his left hand.

Mr. Jenkins pulled into a parking space. Lee grabbed his gi, which he'd ironed the night before and hung on a hanger covered by a clear plastic bag. At a promotion, it was important to look your best.

"I hope you don't mind if I go on ahead," Lee said to his family as he threw open the back door to the jeep. "You coming, Michael?"

Michael nodded. His face looked pale, and his blond hair was damp with sweat even though it was pretty cold out.

"We'll see you after," Lee said, starting to rush towards the dojo.

"Unh unh unh!" his mom said, stepping down to the pavement. "Not so fast."

Lee knew his mom wanted to kiss them for luck. Ordinarily, he didn't mind, but he didn't want to look sappy in front of anybody. Lee checked around the parking lot to make sure none of the visiting black belts were around. All he saw was a woman pushing a baby in a stroller.

"OK," he said, offering his cheek to his mother.

His mom kissed him lightly, then wiped off the lipstick she'd left behind. After she'd kissed Michael, too, Lee and his brother ran towards the dojo.

Lee could barely open the door because the front hallway was so crowded with people. Dwight Vernon was taking off his sneakers while his dad snapped pictures of him with an expensive-looking camera. Lee thought it was funny that Mr. Vernon wanted to photograph Dwight taking off his shoes. On the other hand, Mr. Vernon was a reporter for WMID-TV, the local television station. To him, everything was news.

Lots of adults Lee didn't recognize were also taking off their shoes, but the shoe shelves in the closet near the door were already full.

"Oh well," Lee said, kicking off his sneakers and throwing them on top of a growing pile on the floor of the closet. Then he pushed through the crowd towards the door that led to the classroom. The deck was already filling up with uniformed kids and adults practicing kata in groups according to the color of their belts. Each group had a black belt standing nearby, watching and making corrections. At the back of the classroom, friends and family were sitting on the floor or standing up, watching with awestruck faces or taking pictures with cameras or video cameras.

Michael, right behind Lee, groaned. "I don't know if I can handle this . . ."

"You'll handle it," Lee said, grabbing Michael's arm and pulling him onto the deck. They both bowed to the shinden wall and dodged the relatives and practicing deshi as they made their way to the locker room.

The locker room was so crowded with bodies that Lee couldn't find a hanger for his clothes. There was no room on the bench, either, to sit down. Lee was happy that at least he had his locker. Most of his stuff should fit in there.

Somehow or other, Lee and Michael managed to get dressed and squeeze their way back onto the deck. There were now so many large groups of people doing kata that the groups were starting to bump into each other. Lee spotted his parents and Jeremy standing in the back. Mr. Jenkins was trying to take a picture of Jeremy, but Jeremy kept turning his back. Jeremy didn't look too happy, and Lee understood completely. It must be hard to watch all your friends testing when you weren't allowed, especially when you had a broken hand.

"Brown belts over here," said Sempai Mackay, the chief instructor for the dojo.

Lee punched Michael on the shoulder for luck, and Michael did the same to Lee. Then, with a quick wave to Michael, Lee ran off to join a dozen adults and kids practicing Pinan Sandan, the third green-belt kata. Rosalie Davis was there, even though she wasn't testing. Lee knew she hadn't shown up just because she was Sensei's daughter. It was important to attend all promotions whether you were testing or not. This showed good spirit and support for your fellow deshi. Alyse Walker was there, too, and some adults Lee sort of recognized from the recent outdoor demonstration.

"You'll work half-speed until you're warmed up," said Sempai Mackay. He was in his mid-thirties and had curly black hair and a black mustache. He was Sensei Davis's right-hand man and taught some of the adult classes. He was also responsible for running promotions. This left Sensei Davis free to observe and judge the students who were testing.

"Arigato, Sempai!" Lee shouted, getting in line behind a tall man.

Within minutes, Lee was dripping with sweat, not just because he was working hard. There were so many people in the room, the temperature felt like it had gone up ten degrees! But it was good to be warm. Your muscles were more flexible.

"Shotu-mate!" someone shouted.

Lee, the other brown belts, and all the other deshi instantly stopped whatever they were doing and stood at attention.

"Sensei ni mawate!" shouted the same, unseen person.

Lee turned in the direction of Sensei Davis's office and saw three heads bobbing as they walked onto the deck and stopped. Lee recognized Sensei Davis's sandy hair. The man next to him had thinning hair and a black goatee. Lee had never met this man in person, but he knew him from photographs. It was Sensei Modigliani, Sensei Davis's and Jamie's former teacher from North Carolina. The third was a woman, Sensei Baker. Lee had seen her at some of the other promotions. Sensei Baker, a third-degree black belt, had smooth brown skin, very short gray hair and a lanky frame.

"Sensei ni rei!" the voice shouted.

A hundred bodies tilted forward as they bowed. "Onegai-shimasu, Sensei!" everyone shouted at the top of their lungs.

"Onegai-shimasu," the senseis said, bowing.

The deshi parted, creating a path for the senseis to make their way to the three folding chairs that had been set up for them in front of the shinden wall. The senseis would be the judges for today's promotion.

"Line up, rank order!" Sempai Mackay shouted.

There was a sound like a runaway herd of cattle stampeding as all the deshi ran across the deck, trying to organize themselves by rank.

"Four lines!" Sensei Mackay said.

Four black belts took places right in front of the judges, and everyone lined up right behind them— other black belts, then brown belts with black tips, brown belts, green belts with brown tips, green belts, white belts with green tips, then white belts who'd shown up for their first promotion.

Senseis Davis, Modigliani, and Baker stood in front of their folding chairs, and Sempai Mackay stood off to the side, holding a clipboard. Sensei Davis stepped forward.

"Thank you all for coming," he told everyone in his hoarse, raspy voice. "It's going to be a long day, so pace yourselves and drink plenty of water during the breaks. Before we begin, I'd like to introduce you to some of our distinguished visitors, who've traveled a long way to be here today."

Sensei introduced Sensei Modigliani, Sensei Baker, and a half dozen other senseis and sempais from around the country. The visitors took their bows. Then Sensei Modigliani, the highest-ranking person on the deck, gave the command for everyone to sit in seiza position. A hundred bodies, including the three senseis in the front, dropped to the floor, legs folded beneath them.

Lee closed his eyes, rested his upturned hands on the knot of his belt, and tried to send all the tension and excitement out of his body. *There's nothing special about today,* he tried to tell himself, though he didn't really believe it. *And there's no reason to get nervous. Just do your kata like you would any other day.*

Lee heard the sound of clapping hands. Sensei Modigliani gave the next command. "Shinden ni mawate!"

The judges turned towards the photographs on the wall behind them.

"Shinden ni rei!"

The senseis and all the other deshi dropped their heads to the floor as they bowed to the photographs. After they'd all come up again, the judges turned back to face the class.

"Dozo," Sensei Modigliani said, gesturing to a black belt sensei Lee didn't know.

"Sensei ni rei!" the visited sensei shouted.

"Onegai-shimasu, Sensei!" everyone shouted.

"Class up," Sensei Modigliani said.

Sempai Mackay led everyone in five minutes of warm-ups. Then all the black belts formed a semicircle behind the judges' chairs and Sempai Mackay stepped towards the remaining deshi, carrying his clipboard.

"First group testing for green belt," he said in his clear, precise voice. "When I call your name, come forward. Everyone else move back but stay in rank order."

"Arigato, Sempai!" everyone shouted.

Lee stepped back into the crowd of brown belts and watched as a dozen anxious deshi moved to the front of the room. Adults and kids, they all had white belts with green tips, and they were all testing for green belt. Lee remembered his first promotion. It had been much scarier than his earlier tests for green tips, which you did in a small group after class. This was a much bigger deal. You had to go up in front of all these strangers and try not to make a fool of yourself.

"Everyone else may sit," Sempai Mackay instructed. "White belts, you'll be called one at a time to come before the board and demonstrate the first three kata. Right before it's your turn, I'll let you know you're 'on deck,' so while the person ahead of you is testing, you can warm up in the hall. Understood?"

"Arigato, Sempai!" the nervous white belts shouted.

"First up, Bob DiStanislao. On deck, Caroline Hammersley."

A skinny boy with black hair stood up and faced the judges. A small girl with long blond hair also stood and ducked out the door to the hall. The remaining white belts were all grown-ups.

"Onegai-shimasu!" Bob DiStanislao shouted, stepping forward to face the judges.

Lee watched while the boy demonstrated Fukyugata Ichi, Fukyugata Ni, and Fukyugata San, the first three white-belt kata. His body was tight and tense, but he looked strong and didn't make any mistakes.

After he'd done his kata, the judges told him to step forward while they asked him questions. Sensei Baker asked where their style of karate came from, and the boy correctly answered Okinawa. Sensei Davis asked what the first rule of karate was, and the boy correctly answered *Karate ni sente nashi*. Sensei Modigliani asked the boy how often he trained, and the boy apologetically answered that he came only once a week. Everyone knew you were supposed to come at least twice a week. Sensei Davis told Bob to try to come more often, then Bob got to sit down while Caroline was called up on the spot.

After the white belts had finished testing, the senseis got up from their chairs and Sempai Mackay called "Everybody up!"

Lee's feet and legs tingled as he rose to his feet. The hardest part about promotion, for him, wasn't all the kata you ended up doing but sitting still for so long. Lee's feet always fell asleep.

"Sensei ni rei!" Sempai Mackay shouted.

"Arigato, Sensei!" Everyone shouted, bowing.

The judges filed back into Sensei Davis's office. Lee knew, after so many promotions, what was going on. After each group tested, the judges talked among themselves, deciding who had passed and who hadn't.

Meanwhile, the deshi on deck had to practice Fukyugata Ichi over and over again until the judges came out to watch the next group. The judges didn't announce any of their decisions until the very end of the promotion.

"First kata, Fukyugata Ichi!" Sempai Mackay shouted. "Yo-i!"

It was hard to keep his balance on tingling feet, but Lee managed to get through several dozen repetitions of the kata until the judges returned. Then Sempai Mackay had them bow to the judges and sit down again. People testing for brown tips were up next.

There were over twenty of them. They had to demonstrate the first three white-belt kata, plus the first two Pinan, or green-belt, kata and the first two prearranged fighting sequences. It took over an hour for them to get through. Then the judges disappeared again and the remaining deshi did another couple dozen first kata.

When the senseis returned again, it was to judge the people testing for brown belt. Lee's heart started beating faster when he saw Michael stand up and move to the front of the room with the other green belts with brown tips. Michael still looked pale and nervous. He sat down next to Dwight Vernon, along with the eight other people testing.

"Dwight Vernon, you're up first," said Sempai Mackay. "Michael Jenkins, you're on deck."

Michael stood up again and ran towards the door to the hallway. Just before he disappeared, he shot Lee a panicked look. Lee gave him a thumbs-up, trying to encourage him, but Michael just shook his head. *Poor Michael*, Lee thought. *I hope he doesn't run out of here while he has the chance!*

Dwight ran through his kata looking as relaxed and confident as if he were in a room by himself. In fact, he looked like he was actually enjoying himself! *Leave it to Dwight*, Lee thought. *He loves being the center of attention*. Dwight got one of his answers wrong when the judges asked him a question, but Lee was sure it wouldn't matter. Dwight would pass for sure.

"Michael Jenkins," Sempai Mackay called, adding "Madeline Gonzalez, you're on deck."

Lee looked toward the doorway leading to the hall. There was no sign of Michael. Lee hadn't really believed Michael would run, but now he wasn't so sure. Michael *had* seemed more nervous this morning than he had before any other promotion. Was it possible Michael had chickened out?

Chapter Eleven

"Michael Jenkins?" Sempai Mackay called again.

"Come on, Michael!" Lee whispered. "Don't give up now!"

Michael poked his head in the doorway.

"On the spot," Sempai Mackay said, pointing.

Grimacing, Michael slowly made his way to the center of the floor. "Onegai-shimasu, Sensei!" he said, sounding like he was in pain.

"I'll announce the kata then give the hajime," Sempai Mackay explained. That meant he was just going to tell Michael to begin; he wasn't going to count out every move. "Kata!" he shouted.

"Kata!" Michael shouted back. When you were testing, you had to shout out your kata to show energy and spirit.

"Fukyugata Ichi!" Sempai Mackay shouted.

"Fukyugata Ichi!" Michael answered, bowing.

"Yo-i!"

Michael took the ready position, covering his groin with crossed palms.

"Hajime!" Sempai Mackay gave the command to begin.

Michael's first down block looked wobbly, and his first punch was weak. After that, though, he seemed to gain his footing and power. By the time he was done, Lee breathed a sigh of relief. Whatever had been bothering Michael, he seemed to have gotten over it.

"Fukyugata San," Sempai Mackay said, skipping to the third white-belt kata. People testing for brown belt didn't have to demonstrate every single kata they knew. It wasn't like they were getting away with anything, though. Since no one knew which kata they'd be tested on, they had to know them all.

Michael ran smoothly through the next kata, which demonstrated low stances and double punches. Then Sempai Mackay had him do Pinan Shodan, the first green-belt kata. Michael's cat stance looked strong, and his knife hands flew out like lethal weapons. The rest of his kata looked good, too, and Michael knew the answers to all his questions. By the time Michael sat down, Lee had stopped worrying. Michael would definitely get his brown belt.

After the group testing for brown belt had finished, the judges left the room again. Lee rose shakily to his sleeping feet, stomping on them to wake them up.

His legs were stiff, too, from sitting for so long. But that was nothing compared to the pounding in his head. In just a few minutes, it would be *his* turn to test. It had been almost easy to forget about his own nervousness as he watched everybody else. But now there was nothing else to think about except the fact that he was about to do the hardest thing he'd ever done in his life.

Lee had watched people test for black tips before. It was murder. You had to demonstrate every single kata, the first *three* prearranged fighting sequences, and answer twice as many questions as anybody else. The questions were much harder, too. Black tip students were responsible for teaching all the lower ranks, so they had to prove at promotion that they knew just about everything.

"First kata, Fukyugata Ichi!" Sempai Mackay shouted. "Yo-i!"

The next thirty kata seemed to take no time at all. Then the judges came back into the room and sat down. "People testing for black tips, move forward," Sempai Mackay said.

"Good luck, Lee!" someone whispered.

Lee turned and saw Jamie Oscarson, sitting a few feet away from him. He hadn't noticed her before, with all the people, and he hadn't thought about her either, with everything else on his mind. But seeing her now didn't make him feel angry or inferior. It just reminded him how good he could be if he just worked hard enough.

"Thanks," Lee whispered back, stepping forward. Four brown belt adults filled in on either side of him.

"Lee Jenkins, you're first," Sempai Mackay said. "Brett Pierce, you're on deck. Everyone else, be seated."

Thump! Thump! Thump! Lee's heart was beating so fast and loud he was sure everyone in the dojo could hear it. The three judges stared at him with no expression on their faces. Lee tried not to think about how many years they'd been training and how good they were. He tried not to think about how inexperienced he'd look in their eyes. He tried not to think at all.

Jamie's voice echoed in his head, giving him courage. *After all the time you've put in, the moves are in your body. The best thing is to not even think and just do it on auto-pilot.*

Jamie was right. Lee had nothing to worry about. After all the years he'd studied, he was bound to pass. He was ready.

Lee bowed low to the judges. "Onegai-shimasu, Sensei!" he shouted at the top of his lungs.

"Fukyugata Ichi," Sempai Mackay commanded. "No count. Yo-i!"

Lee took the ready position.

"Hajime!"

Lee flowed from one kata to another, but his mind wasn't completely empty. He thought about Jamie's technique and tried to incorporate it into his. He copied her low stances and quick sharp movements. He copied the snap of her hips and her utter relaxation between moves. As Lee progressed to the more advanced kata, he stopped worrying. His kata were better than they'd ever been before. But this wasn't over yet. They'd tested his body. Now they were going to test his mind.

"Arigato, Sensei!" Lee shouted when he was done. He was gasping for breath, and his soaking wet gi was dripping puddles on the floor.

"Approach the judges," Sempai Mackay said.

Lee stepped forward. It was time to answer questions.

Sensei Baker nodded at Lee. "In the first kata, Fukyugata Ichi," she began, "which move is a kiai move?"

This was a trick question. Lee knew because he'd heard it asked many times at previous promotions. In the first kata, there was one move, a walking punch, where you "kiaied," shouting as loud as you could when you threw the punch. But kiai wasn't just the shout. Kiai was pouring every bit of strength and power you had into a move, and you were supposed to do that all the time, whether you shouted or not.

"All moves are kiai moves, Sensei," Lee said respectfully, bowing.

"Who composed Fukyugata Ichi?" Sensei Baker asked.

"Shoshin Nagamine," Lee answered. Nagamine was the master in Okinawa who had developed their style of karate.

"Arigato," Sensei Baker said.

Lee bowed and moved on to Sensei Modigliani. He knew from watching other promotions that the questions were going to get harder and harder.

"What is the most important move in a kata?" Sensei Modigliani asked.

Lee bit his lip. Sensei hadn't said *which* kata, and there were so many moves. Lee thought hard. Maybe Sensei wasn't talking about one kata in particular. So what was the general rule? Then Lee figured out the answer. "The move you are doing at the moment is the most important one," he said.

"Arigato," said Sensei Modigliani.

Lee moved on to Sensei Davis.

"What is the meaning of the word *karate*?" Sensei Davis asked.

"*Karate* is Japanese for empty hand," Lee explained. "*Kara* means empty, and *te* means hand."

"And why do we fight with empty hands?" Sensei Davis asked.

"Our style of karate originated in Okinawa," Lee said. "When the Okinawans were conquered by Japanese war lords, they were forbidden to carry weapons. So they developed a style of self-defense using their bodies, their empty hands, as weapons."

Sensei Davis nodded. Then he asked his final question.

"Can you recite the karate creed?" Sensei Davis asked.

Lee gulped. He'd heard the creed a few times, and he'd read it in one of the karate books he'd bought at the dojo, but he'd never tried to memorize it. What should he do? If he got it wrong, it might cost him everything. On the other hand, if he didn't even try, he wouldn't be showing spirit. Lee had no choice but to give it a shot. He remembered the beginning, at least.

"I come to you only with karate," Lee began hesitantly. "My hands are empty, but I fear no man . . ."

What came after that? Something about defending yourself. *Come on!* he prodded himself. *Try to remember! Pretend the book is open in front of you. Just read it!* Then, a miracle happened. Lee could almost see the book floating in the air in front of his eyes, open to the right page. All he had to do was read the words out loud.

"Should I be forced to defend myself, my honor, or my principles," Lee went on, "should it be a matter

137

of right or wrong, life or death—then here are my weapons—my empty hands."

Sensei actually smiled! Lee breathed a deep sigh of relief. His body suddenly felt very light.

"Arigato," Sensei said.

Lee snapped smartly to attention. "Arigato, Sensei!" he shouted.

Lee barely saw what happened after that. He'd made it! The fact that those words had come to him out of nowhere was definitely a sign that he'd passed.

After the last person had tested, the black belts set up cement blocks and boards. Lee had been so happy, he'd almost forgotten about breaking. It wasn't as important as kata, and it didn't matter whether you broke the boards or not, but you had to show spirit and at least try. For the lower ranks testing, the black belts set up two boards. Almost everybody broke, and almost everyone who did seemed very surprised and pleased. Michael managed to break three boards. Then it was Lee's turn.

Sempai Seeger, one of the adult black belts from the dojo, stacked four boards between the concrete blocks.

Lee stepped forward. He'd never broken four boards before. He wouldn't have been that scared, though, if Jeremy hadn't just broken his hand trying to do the same thing. But Jeremy hadn't been ready to break such a big stack. Lee was. He hoped.

Lee took a low squatting stance and raised his knife hand high above his head. He tried to picture his hand not hitting the boards but going right through them. But his hand wasn't a hand anymore. It was the world's sharpest knife.

"Hyaaaah!" Lee kiaied.

He didn't even feel the boards as he sank to one knee. It was almost like the boards had jumped apart to let his hand through. They now lay on the floor in eight even pieces.

Everyone applauded.

"Very good, Lee," Sempai Seeger said, picking up the broken boards.

After breaking, it was time for demonstrations. This was where students demonstrated kata, bunkai, and weapons. The adult brown belt men did *Naihanshi Sho* while black belts walked up and down in front of them, punching them in the legs and arms to test their endurance. A few of the visiting senseis demonstrated *nunchuku* kata, whipping short wooden sticks around so fast and hard that they made whistling sounds in the air.

Lee was enjoying just being a spectator until Sensei Davis called Jamie Oscarson up by herself. Jamie stepped forward, carrying a *bo,* a five-foot-long wooden stick that was taller than she was. Lee was confused. There were plenty of other kids and adults who studied the bo. Why had Sensei asked her to demonstrate all by herself?

"I'd like to introduce you all to our newest student," Sensei Davis said as Jamie stood quietly at attention, facing the audience. She held her bo upright beside her. "Jamie Oscarson has just recently moved here from North Carolina where she studied under Sensei Modigliani. We are very happy to welcome her to our dojo, and I think we can all learn something by watching her."

"Arigato, Sensei!" Jamie shouted, bowing.

Jamie started her bo kata, lunging and stabbing and whipping the wooden staff around so quickly and so effortlessly that the bo started to sing. Lee had never seen anything like it in his life. It wasn't just that her hands were loose as she threw and recaught the bo over and over again. It wasn't that her techniques looked deadly and beautiful. The unbelievable part was that it seemed like Jamie had disappeared. She wasn't a girl doing a kata. She *was* the kata. The bo had come alive.

When Jamie finished, the applause was deafening. Sensei Modigliani rose to his feet, and so did Sensei Baker. The black belts, standing behind the judges, looked dumbfounded as if they'd never seen anything like Jamie, either.

Jamie bowed without smiling and went to return

her bo to the weapons wall where the other weapons were hanging.

Lee's heart sank into the floor. The kata he'd just performed, the kata he'd been so proud of, now seemed pathetic. Sure, he'd copied Jamie, but he was just a poor imitation. He'd been kidding himself to think he could be as good as her someday. Sensei Davis must have realized that, too. That was why Sensei had put Jamie on the spot. Sensei had been trying to teach Lee, and everybody else, a lesson.

Lee wanted to excuse himself, to go into the locker room, get dressed, and leave the dojo forever. But he couldn't do that. Whether or not he ended up quitting karate after all, he had to at least stick it out.

The judges rose and went into Sensei Davis's office for the last time. In just a few minutes, they'd return with their final verdict. Lee practiced Fukyugata Ichi again and again and again. He tried to put some energy into it, but his body felt wooden. He'd given his all, and now he had nothing left.

Lee began to lose track of the time. His arms and legs kept doing kata, but Lee felt like he'd lost touch with his body, too. How long were the judges planning to stay in there? Why hadn't they come to any decision? Was it all because of Jamie? Had they decided not to promote *anyone* and now they were figuring out how to break it to people? That had to be it. The judges knew they were about to make an unpopular decision and they didn't know how to handle it.

"Shotu-mate!" called Sempai Mackay.

At last! Lee tiredly drew his body up to attention as Sensei Davis came back out onto the deck, followed by the other senseis.

"Sensei ni rei!" called Sempai Mackay.

"Onegai-shimasu, Sensei!" said a hundred weary voices.

"Onegai-shimasu," said Sensei Davis, bowing. "The judges have made their decision."

Chapter Twelve

"Please be seated," said Sensei Davis.

Lee dropped back down to the floor. He felt like an elevator. Up and down. Up and down.

"In general," said Sensei Davis when everyone was comfortable, "you were a strong group. I saw some very good kata, sharp techniques, and a lot of spirit . . ."

But . . . ? Lee could tell by the way Sensei Davis began that there was a "but" coming. He was probably going to say that he'd been wrong all along. With a girl like Jamie Oscarson at the dojo, there really *was* no need to have any other students.

". . . but that doesn't mean everyone will be given their new rank today," Sensei went on.

Lee had seen it coming. That was Sensei's way of saying some or maybe all the students had failed.

"If you are not promoted today," Sensei said, "you should not consider it a failure. It's merely an indication that you must train even harder. I know some of you will probably feel discouraged, but try to think of this as a challenge. Now, when I call your name, please come forward." Sempai Mackay handed Sensei Davis his clipboard. "Bob DiStanislao," Sensei Davis read.

People applauded as the first white belt who'd tested ran to the front of the classroom. Sensei Davis pulled a green belt and a large white envelope out of a brown cardboard box. Lee knew the envelope contained Bob's certificate announcing that he'd been promoted. He was surprised that Sensei had promoted anybody, but maybe he shouldn't have been. Sensei couldn't really fail everybody. He'd have to close the dojo. But that still didn't mean Lee had passed.

When Bob DiStanislao reached the front of the room, first he shook Sensei Baker's hand, then Sensei Modigliani's hand, and Sensei Davis's hand. Sensei Davis handed him the envelope and the belt.

Sensei continued reading off the clipboard. All but two of the white belts had been promoted. Two of the people testing for brown tips weren't called to the front either. It looked like Sensei was failing more people than he usually did. Some years, everybody passed. But that was before Jamie Oscarson.

"Dwight Vernon," Sensei Davis called.

"Yes!!!!" Dwight shouted, pumping his fist and leaping into the air.

"That's my baby!" Mrs. Vernon shouted while her husband snapped a few million pictures.

At the word "baby," Dwight turned towards the back where his parents were sitting. "Thanks a lot, Mom," he shouted, but he didn't look angry. He was too happy about getting his brown belt. Dwight sprinted to the front of the room and vigorously shook the hands of all the judges.

"Michael Jenkins," Sensei called.

Lee felt a cheer rise in his throat. Even though he was sure that he'd failed, he was still really happy for his brother. Michael had worked hard and he deserved to advance.

Mr. Jenkins scooted forward through the seated students to snap a picture of Michael shaking Sensei Davis's hand. In the back, Mrs. Jenkins was wiping her eyes with a tissue. Jeremy was slapping his left hand against his thigh, trying to applaud.

After Michael received his brown belt, Sensei Davis announced the rest of the names of people who'd tested for that rank. All but one person passed. Lee tried not to get hopeful, but he couldn't help it. If all these lower-ranking students had passed, maybe he had a chance, too. Lee waited, listening for his name, but Sensei said nothing. He merely scanned the list on his clipboard and whispered something to Sensei Modigliani.

Uh-oh, Lee thought. The worst had happened. Sensei had passed the lower-ranking students because they didn't have to take as much responsibility for the dojo. They were still learning. But at black-tip level, the standards were much higher, especially with Jamie to set the example. Lee understood now, though. Until someone could be as good as Jamie, he or she didn't deserve to pass.

"Lee!" Jamie hissed, nudging him. "Go on!"

Lee turned to Jamie in confusion. "Huh?" he asked.

"He's calling you!" she whispered.

"Lee Jenkins?" Sensei Davis asked. "Are you still here?"

Not understanding, Lee threaded through the white uniformed bodies until he'd reached the front of the classroom. Sensei Baker extended her hand and shook his. "Congratulations," she said with a smile.

Lee stepped to the left to shake Sensei Modigliani's hand. "Congratulations," said the fifth-degree black belt.

Then Sensei Davis handed Lee an envelope. "Congratulations," he said.

Lee wandered back into the crowd. Why had the judges been congratulating him? He hadn't been promoted. It just wasn't possible. Still, he was curious to see what was in the envelope. Maybe it was a letter

from Sensei encouraging him to stick with karate anyway.

Lee tore open the white paper and pulled out two
black pockets of cloth. They sure looked like black
tips. Lee pulled out the certificate, just to make sure.
There it was, written in beautiful italic letters:

This is to certify that

Lee Jenkins

has been promoted to

Black Tips

at the Midvale Karate Dojo

in accordance with

the regulation of this karate school.

Signed by

Ansei Ueshiro, Grand Master

There was no denying it now. Lee really *had*
passed. But there had to be some mistake!

"Thank you all for coming," Sensei Davis con-
cluded. "You are dismissed."

"Arigato, Sensei!" everyone shouted, bowing. Then
the room went wild. Everyone was laughing and
cheering and hugging each other.

"Hey, Lee!" Michael said, slapping him on the
back. "Way to go! You looked great up there!"

"You too," Lee said, trying to sound as enthusiastic as Michael. "Congratulations!"

"Where are my two ninja warriors?" Mrs. Jenkins asked, pushing towards her sons. She hugged Lee and kissed him on the cheek with a big smack.

While Mrs. Jenkins turned to kiss Michael, Mr. Jenkins shook Lee's hand. "I'm proud of you," he said warmly, shaking Lee's hand. "Put your new belt on so I can take a picture."

"Uh, I can't," Lee said, showing his father the tips. "These have to be sewn to the belt." *And I'm not putting these on until I talk to Sensei Davis,* he added to himself. How could he wear his black tips when he really didn't deserve them? Lee was convinced, now, that Sensei Davis had made a mistake, and it was up to Lee to clear things up.

Sensei Davis passed by, heading towards his office. Sensei was probably very busy with all his visitors, but Lee had to try to talk to him. If he didn't, he'd explode!

"Sensei!" Lee called after him, but his voice was drowned out by the happily chattering crowd. "Sensei!"

Sensei Davis turned as he reached the doorway to his office. "Hi, Lee," he said. Then he noticed Lee's expression. "Is something wrong?"

"I think so," Lee said hesitantly. "I think there may have been a mistake."

Sensei bowed to the shinden wall, then held open the curtain to his office. "Come in," he said.

Lee bowed to the shinden and followed Sensei inside.

"Sit down, Lee," Sensei said, taking a seat behind his desk. "What's on your mind?"

It was hard to talk with various black belts rushing in and out of the room, but Lee had to get this off his chest. "I don't get it," Lee said, sitting down on the hard wooden chair. "I don't understand why I passed. Jamie's so much better than I am. It doesn't matter how many years I study or how many hours I practice every day. I'll never be as good as her."

Sensei frowned. "I guess you didn't understand what I was trying to tell you before."

"I guess not," Lee said, feeling his face grow hot. He seemed to be missing the point of everything these days.

"Let me tell you a story," Sensei said. He leaned back in his chair and rested his hands on the knot of his black belt.

"A young boy traveled across Japan to the school of a famous martial artist. When he arrived at the dojo, he was given an audience by the sensei.

" 'What do you wish from me?' the master asked.

" 'I wish to be your student and become the finest karateka in the land,' the boy replied. 'How long must I study?'

" 'Ten years at least,' the master answered.

" 'Ten years is a long time,' said the boy. 'What if I studied twice as hard as all your other students?'

" 'Twenty years,' replied the master.

" 'Twenty years! What if I practice day and night with all my effort?'

" 'Thirty years,' was the master's reply.

" 'How is it that each time I say I will work harder, you tell me that it will take longer?' the boy asked.

" 'The answer is clear. When one eye is fixed upon your destination, there is only one eye left with which to find the Way.' "

"Do you understand the story?" Sensei asked Lee. Lee tried to make sense of it. "It seems like the harder he worked, the longer it would take, but I don't see why."

"Let's put it another way," Sensei said. "Do you know the difference between karate and karate-do?"

Lee had studied that when he was practicing for the question-and-answer part of the promotion. "Karate is an empty-handed martial art," Lee said, quoting

the book he'd read. "Karate-do is the w
living your whole life by karate principle

"That's what the book says," Sensei re
"But karate-do is a lot more than that. The
always be people who are better than you or w
than you. But that's not the important thing."

Sensei drew in a deep breath, and fixed his dark
eyes on Lee.

"The most important thing," Sensei said, "is to remember that there are many paths up the mountain,
and they all lead to the same place."

Lee was starting to see. "So what you're saying is
that Jamie's path isn't *my* path, so I don't have to race
her to the top?"

Sensei Davis smiled. "Exactly. It's up to each person to find his or her own path. And it's the path itself,
the way, that's the essence of karate. Not the destination."

Vanity is the only obstacle to life.

—Funakoshi

Arigato—Thank you

Bo—Weapon. Wooden staff with tapered ends

Bunkai—Application of kata where one or more actual opponents demonstrate attacking techniques

Cat stance—Body weight rests on the bent back leg, front foot lightly touches the floor. Most advantageous for attacking an opponent's side

Chishi—Wooden handle with weight attached, used to develop upper-body strength

Dai-sho—Two samurai swords, one short and one long

Deshi—Karate student

Dojo—Sacred hall of learning; karate school

Down block—Downward strike with forearm, used against attack aimed at lower body

Dozo—Please

Fukyugata Ichi—First white-belt kata composed of

walking and reverse punches, down blocks and high blocks. Most basic kata

Gi—Karate uniform

Hajime—Begin

Jyu-kumite—Freestyle sparring

Karate—Weaponless form of self-defense. Literally means "empty (*kara*) hand (*te*)"

Karate-do—The "way" of karate; karate as not only a martial art but a philosophy, a way of life

Karate ni sente nashi—There is no first attack in karate

Kata—Form. An organized series of pre-arranged defensive and offensive movements symbolizing an imaginary fight between several opponents and performed in a geometrical pattern. Handed down and perfected by karate masters

Kendo—The way of the sword

Kiai—Concentration of energy and power in one sharp burst, sometimes accompanied by a loud shout used to startle opponent

Kime—Tension at moment of impact for maximum power

Kimono—Japanese robe

Kio-tsuke—Attention

Knife hands—Four fingers straight and pressed stiffly together, thumb pressed in tightly. Side of hand used to slash or strike an opponent

Ma-ai—Sense of proper distance from an opponent

Makiwara—Striking post, used to toughen knuckles and hands

Mawate—Turn

Naihanchi Sho—First brown-belt kata, featuring wide-legged "horse" stance. Trains lower parts of the body

Nunchuku—Flail (a weapon). Two wooden sticks connected by a rope

Onegai-shimasu—Please teach me

Pinan Nidan—Second green-belt kata

Pinan Sandan—Third green-belt kata

Pinan Shodan—First green-belt kata. Introduces cat stance and knife-hand techniques

Reverse punch—Punching fist is on the opposite side of forward leg

Rei—Bow

Sai—Slender pointed weapon resembling sword

Samurai—Japanese warrior

Seiza—Folded-leg sitting position

Sempai—Senior student

Sensei—Teacher or master

Sensei ni mawate—Turn to Sensei

Sensei ni rei—Bow to Sensei

Shinden—Old masters, ancient and past teachers of karate

Shotu-mate—Stop, be quiet

Shugo—Line up

Solar plexus—Nerve center located beneath the rib
    cage. A vulnerable target
Te—Hand
Walking punch—Punching fist is on the same side
    as forward leg
Yame—Stop
Yo-i—Ready

COUNTING

Ichi—One
Ni—Two
San—Three
Shi—Four
Go—Five
Roku—Six
Shichi—Seven
Hachi—Eight
Ku—Nine
Ju—Ten

Carin Greenberg Baker has written many books for young readers but claims the Karate Club series is her favorite. "I'm a deshi, too," she says, "and writing about karate is another way to help me learn more." She has studied karate for several years at the dojo owned by her husband, Sensei David Baker, and recently earned the rank of green belt with brown tips. When she's not practicing karate or writing about it, she serves as the co-headwriter of *Ghostwriter,* a weekly television series on PBS.